Yun Heung-gil

THE HOUSE OF TWILIGHT

Edited with an Introduction by

Martin Holman

readers international

© Yun Heung-gil 1989

Published in English by Readers International, Inc., and Readers International, London. Editorial inquiries to London office at 8 Strathray Gardens, London NW3 4NY, England. US/Canadian inquiries to Subscriber Service Department, P.O. Box 959, Columbia, LA 71418-0959 USA.

Readers International and the editor gratefully acknowledge the help of Suh Ji-moon, Bruce and Ju-chan Fulton, and the late Ch'oe Hae-ch'un who gave permission for their works to be included in this volume.
Cover art and frontispiece from Korean edition of Yun Hueng-gil's stories, used courtesy of the author.
Cover design by Jan Brychta
Typesetting by Emset, London NW10 UK

Printed in Malta by Interprint Limited.

Library of Congress Catalog Card Number: 88-63256

British Library Cataloguing in Publication Data

Yun, Heung-gil
   The House of Twilight: Stories by Yun Heung-gil
   I. Title   II. Holman, Martin

ISBN 0-930523-59-8 Hardcover
ISBN 0-930523-60-1 Paperback

Шапик. 1979.

Contents

Introduction
by Martin Holman

Yun Heung-gil was born in Chollabukdo Province in the southern part of Korea in 1942, while Korea was still under Japanese colonial rule, as it had been since 1910. He was in the second grade when the Korean War began and witnessed the internecine struggle as a child, a viewpoint he was later to adopt in a number of his best stories.

In 1958 Yun entered a teachers' college. The postwar years were hard and turbulent as the increasingly dictatorial aims of the South Korean president Syngman Rhee became more apparent. Yun was a junior in college when the April 19, 1960 student uprising forced Rhee from power. The subsequent democratic government was soon overthrown by Park Chung-hee, who was to rule Korea until his assassination in 1979. During those still unsettled times, Yun served in the Korean Air Force for three years, after which he finally took up his first teaching position at an elementary school.

Yun's writing soon attracted attention. In 1966 he won a new writers' prize from a literary magazine, and, two years later, his story "The Season of the Gray Crown" received the first place award in a prestigious competition sponsored by the *Hanguk Ilbo* newspaper. Since then Yun has won a number of other literary prizes and is regarded as one of the rising stars in Korean literature. His work has also found audiences outside Korea. Besides English, his work has also appeared in French and German, and he has the distinction of being the most widely read Korean writer in Japan, where two of his novels and two short story collections have been published in Japanese translation. After a difficult period of writing while supporting himself and his family with teaching and other jobs, Yun has, for the last ten years, been able to devote himself full time to writing.

During the politically turbulent '80's — an era that has seen the rise of another military ruler, popular cries for democracy that have brought reform, and the emergence of Korea on the international scene as an economic power — Yun's literary output has continued to be impressive. "The House of Twilight," "The Rainy Spell," and "The Man Who Was Left as Nine Pairs of Shoes" were each the title story of one of Yun's several collections. His novels *Mother*, *The Sea of Apocalypse*, and others have also been well received.

Yun Heung-gil was only eight years old when the Korean War broke out. He witnessed the fabric of his nation rent by conflicting ideologies, and, in his literature, he has portrayed families ravaged by those clashes both from within and without. But because his narrators are often children, the ideological struggle is presented obliquely. The narrator sees the conflicts only on the most basic human level and is either unaware or unconvinced of the magnitude or the import of the ideologies his elders may espouse. His child-narrators make no arguments for or against one system or another, but, by its nature, Yun's work offers a powerful argument for the dignity of human life. His characters may be riddled with flaws and weaknesses, but Yun's perspective will not allow them to be unduly vilified or exalted. His even-handed touch reveals the richness of his characters, who are possessed of both good and evil in great proportions.

Like so many other young Korean writers who made their debuts in the '60s and '70s, Yun also concerns himself with the inequities of the contemporary social and economic system in rapidly industrializing Korea, where many appear to be left out of the much-touted "economic miracle" and fall victim to the oppressive excesses — purposeful or inadvertent — of society. In his stories set in contemporary Korea, as in those of the Korean War, Yun takes pains to illuminate his characters from multiple angles, to seek the necessary complexities within them. Indeed one of his chief concerns is the tragedy of misunderstanding, both public and private.

In "The Rainy Spell," the confrontation between the old women that threatens to divide the family asunder is precipitated by a slip of the tongue that may or may not have been intentional, but the two are finally reconciled at something close to a primordial level with a mutual recognition and acknowledgement of their roles as mothers. In "The House of Twilight," the half-crazed woman who lost her home and status after Korea's liberation from the Japanese and her young daughter display what appears to be a mutual, murderous hatred; however, circumstances may have caused them to misdirect the rage they feel, just as fellow villagers have misjudged them. Although the narrator in "The Man Who Was Left Behind as Nine Pairs of Shoes" attempts to be fair and understanding about his renter's plight, he inadvertently drives him away. And in "Gang Beating," callous rumors in a tearoom plague a mysterious young worker.

Yun's literature acknowledges the nagging question of moral responsibility toward our fellow man. Ignorance, purposeful or not, cannot relieve Yun's characters of their burden. His literature does not sermonize, but the moments of recognition in which his characters comprehend at least a portion of that part they play in the lives of others raise questions for the reader as well. As Prof. Suh Ji-moon has explained, "[Yun's] stories, therefore, are not mere chronicles of survival but sincere quests into the problem of how life can be lived at all and how it can be lived meaningfully."

Yun's literary quest benefits greatly from his masterful style and his powerful and symbolic imagery. His stories are enriched by sensory impressions that reinforce his narrative, and thematic concerns are amplified and echoed in his images: the "long, wearying" rainy season, as inescapable and unrelenting as the war, and the pervasive wet barley spread out to dry on every available surface; the close, clinging, viscous quality of the seductive and mysterious darkness that the boy anticipates in "The House of Twilight"; the view of the sky from the grave-like hole the boy's father digs in "Fuel"; the row of polished shoes — a man's appeal for recognition of his own human dignity. Yun's evocative style attests to his mastery of the storyteller's art.

Yun is a writer both in and out of his time. His work reflects the tribulations Korea has suffered in the years since the end of World War II and Korea's liberation from Japanese domination. His characters endure the buffetings of war, political unrest, disorienting (and dis-Orienting) changes in a society in a whirlwind rush toward modernization. But Yun also depicts the ageless, universal human desire to seek what is worthy in human existence, and his literature reveals both the beauty and tragedy of the quest. He is a writer for Korea and the world.

Berkeley, March 1989

The House of Twilight

The Rainy Spell

1

The rain that had started to pour from the day after we reaped the last pea-pods showed no sign of lifting even after many days. The rain came sometimes in fine powdery drops, or in hard, fierce balls, threatening to pierce the roof. Tonight, rain enveloped the pitch darkness like a dripping-wet mop.

It must have been somewhere right outside the village. My guess is that it was from somewhere around the empty house beside the riverbank which was used for storing funeral palanquins. The house always struck me as an eerie place, and I thought that near it even ordinary dogs would bark in long, dismal, fox-like howls. But it might have been in reality a place much further than the empty house. The relative silence allowed by the thinning rain was being filled by the distant howling of dogs. As if that far-off wail had been a military signal, all the village dogs that had managed to survive the war began to bark in turn. The dogs were unusually fierce that night.

That evening we were gathered in the guest room occupied by my maternal grandmother, because she was greatly disturbed by something, and we all had to comfort and reassure her. But Mother and Maternal Aunt ceased trying to say comforting things after the dogs began to bark outside. Stealing glances at Grandmother, Mother and Aunt were repeatedly turning their eyes towards the darkness beyond, separated from the room only by the door panelled with gauze mosquito net. A nameless moth had been crawling up and down the doorpost with tremulous wings for a long time now.

"Just wait and see. It won't be long till we'll know for sure. Just wait and see if I'm ever wrong," Grandmother murmured in her sunken voice. She was shelling peas from the pods. The peas were to be cooked with the rice for breakfast the next day. Sitting with the lap of her skirt full of damp pea-pods, she shelled the peas with sure, experienced hands — first breaking off the tip and slitting open the pod, then running her finger through it. When the bright green peas slid out to one side, Grandmother cupped them in her palm and poured them into the bamboo basket at her knee, and let the empty pod fall back into her lap.

Mother and Aunt, who lost the chance to make a rejoinder to Grandmother's words, exchanged awkward glances. The rain grew roughly noisy again outside, and the dogs barked more fiercely, as if in competition. The night grew still more stormy, and there came from the direction of the storage platform a clattering of metal hitting the cement floor. It must have been the tin pail hung on the wall. A sudden gust of wind and rain rushed into the room, rattling the door, and blew out the kerosene lamp that had been shivering precariously. The room sank under the sudden flood of darkness and sticky humidity, and the tremor of the moth's wings also stopped. The dog began to bark three or four houses beyond ours in the alley. Our dog Wolly, who had kept silent till then, emitted a growl. The wild commotion of the dogs, which had begun at the entrance of the village, was coming nearer and nearer our house.

"Light that lamp," Grandmother said. "Light the lamp, I said. Didn't you hear me?" Grandmother made a rustle, feeling about the room in the darkness. "What evil weather!"

I groped about the room, found a match, and lit the kerosene lamp. Mother trimmed the wick. A strip of sooty smoke curled upward and drew a round shadow on the ceiling.

"It's always wet like this around this time of the year." Mother spoke in an effort to lessen the unease created by the weather.

"It's all because of the weather. It's because of this weather that you're worrying yourself sick for no reason," Aunt also put in. Aunt had graduated from a high school in Seoul before the war broke out, while my mother's family lived in Seoul.

"No. It isn't for no reason. You don't know. When has my dream ever predicted wrong?" Grandmother shook her head left and right. But even when her head shook, her hands did their work surely and steadily.

"I don't believe in dreams. It was only the day before yesterday we received Kil-jun's letter saying he's well and strong."

"That's right. You read yourself where Kil-jun said he's bored these days because there aren't any battles."

"All that's of no use. I knew three or four days beforehand when your father died. Only, that time, it was a thumb instead of a tooth. I'd dreamed that time my thumb just came loose and disappeared."

Oh, the hateful account of that dream again! Doesn't Grandmother ever get fed up with talking about that dream? Ever since she woke up at dawn, Grandmother had kept murmuring about her dream, her eyes vague and clouded. Continually moving her sunken, almost toothless mouth, she kept hinting that there was an inauspicious force rushing towards her. She had only seven teeth left in all; she had dreamed that a large iron pincer from out of nowhere forced itself into her mouth, yanked the strongest of the seven, and fled. The first thing Grandmother did as soon as she woke up from the dream and collected her wits was to feel in her mouth and check the number of her teeth. Then she ordered Aunt to bring a mirror and checked the number again with her eyes. Not content, she made me come right up to her face and demanded from me repeated assurances. No matter how often anybody looked in, there were seven teeth in her mouth, just as before. Moreover, the lower canine tooth that she cherished as a substitute for a grinder was as soundly in its place as ever.

But Grandmother wouldn't give credence to anybody's testimony. It seemed that to her it was out of the question that the canine tooth could remain there as if nothing had happened. Her thoughts were not in reality anymore, but dwelling in her dream. She refused to believe that her daughters and her son-in-law were telling her the truth, and she even doubted the eyesight of her grandson, whom she always praised highly for being good at threading needles. To say nothing of disbelieving the mirror, she even disbelieved her own fingers, which had made a tactile survey of her teeth inside her mouth.

Grandmother had spent the whole long summer's day murmuring about her dream. It taxed all of our nerves to distraction. The first one to break down and mention my maternal uncle's name was my mother. When Mother incautiously mentioned the name of her brother, serving at the front as a major and commander of a platoon in the Republic's army, Grandmother's flabby cheeks convulsed in a spasm. Aunt cast a reproachful look toward her elder sister. Grandmother, however, ignored Mother's words. Before long Aunt also began talking of Uncle, judging that there was no other way of setting the old woman's mind at ease. But Grandmother never uttered her only son's name even once. She just kept on talking about that hateful dream.

From the time darkness began to set in, it became difficult to tell who was being comforted and who was giving comfort. As night deepened, Grandmother's words became more and more darkly suggestive, as if she were under a spell, and her face even took on an expression of triumphant self-confidence. Mother and Aunt, on the other hand, fidgeted uneasily, and gazed vacantly at the pea-pods they had brought in to shell. In the end, all work was handed over to Grandmother, and Mother and Aunt could do nothing but listen to the endless incantatory mutterings of the old woman.

The rain was coming down over the whole surface of the village like a wet mop. The three or four dogs that were lucky enough to survive the war mercilessly tore the shroud of darkness, filling every space with their shrill howls. Grandmother kept on shelling with expert hands, putting the bright green peas into the bamboo basket and the empty pods back into her lap. Our dog Wolly, who received no kindly attention from anybody these difficult, gloomy days, began barking in surprisingly furious and ringing tones. Just then we could hear footsteps rounding the walls of the house next door. They were not the footsteps of just one person. There seemed to be three, or two at least. A foot must have stepped in a puddle; there was a splashing sound, and hard upon it came a grumbling about the evil weather.

Who could those people be, who would dare trudge through the village in this pouring rain in the depth of the night? It was still a dangerous time, even though the war front had receded north, what with the communist partisans still occasionally invading and setting fire to the town police station. No one with any sense of propriety ever visited other people's houses after dark, unless on some emergency. To which house, then, could those people be going at this time of the night? What mischief might they be brewing, tramping the night streets in a group?

Mother grabbed hold of Aunt's hand. Aunt, leaving her hand to her sister's disposal, was staring into the darkness beyond, thinly veiled by the gauze panels of the door. Underneath the wooden porch adjoining the inner room Wolly was vomiting desperate barks. Even Grandmother, whose hearing was not very good, had already realized that the band of men had stopped in front of the twig gate of our house and was hesitating there.

"Here they are at last. Here they are," Grandmother murmured in a parched voice.

"Soon-ku!" Someone called Father's name from beyond the twig gate. "Soon-ku, are you at home?"

In the inner room Paternal Grandmother coughed short- breathed coughs. We could hear Father stirring to go out. Hearing that, Mother whispered frightenedly towards the inner room, "I'll slip out and see what's going on. You stay where you are like a dead body."

But Father was already in the hall. Putting on his shoes, Father bade us the same thing Mother had told him to do. We were ordered by Father never to stir a step from where we were. Wolly, who had been yelping frantically, suddenly ceased barking with a sharp groan. Father must have done something to him. Crossing the yard, Father spoke cautiously, "Who is it?"

"It's me, the village head."

"Why, what brings you here in the middle of the night?"

The bell attached to the twig gate tinkled. We could hear the men exchanging a few words. Then there was silence again outside, and only the vigorous dripping of rain filled our ears. Mother, who had been standing irresolutely in the room, could stand it no longer and threw open the door. She rushed outside, and Aunt followed hurriedly. In the inner room Paternal Grandmother was retching a few short-breathed coughs. Right beside me Maternal Grandmother was shelling peas steadily, completely absorbed in the work. Running her finger through the pod, she murmured, "It won't shake me a bit. I knew we were going to have some tidings today or tomorrow. I knew from long before. I'm all prepared."

I couldn't sit still. After some inner struggle, I left Maternal Grandmother alone and stole out of the room. I could hear her parched voice even on the dirt verandah, "I'm not shaken, not I."

It was much darker outside than I had thought. Each time I moved my legs, Wolly's wet, furry, smelly body hit my inner thighs. The dog kept groaning and licking my hand. The rain was thicker than I had expected when indoors. It bathed my face and soaked my hemp shirt, and made me drenched as a rat that has fallen into a water-jar. Wolly gave up following me any further and retreated, growling fearfully. The grown-ups revealed their outline only when I approached quite close to the twig gate. It looked as if whatever information had to be exchanged was exchanged. The grown-ups just stood still, in spite of the pouring rain. I could dimly see the heads of two men covered with military waterproof cloth and the familiar face of the village head who was standing facing us. Father and Aunt were supporting from either side Mother's trembling, sinking body. After a long silence the village head spoke.

"Please give your mother-in-law my sincere condolences."

Then one of the two men shrouded under the military waterproof cloth spoke. He hesitated a great deal, as if extremely reluctant to speak. His voice, therefore, sounded very shy.

"I really don't know what to say. We're just as grieved as any of his family. It was an errand we'd have been glad to be spared. Goodbye, then, sir. We'll have to go back now."

"Thank you. Be careful in the dark," Father said.

They slid through the twig gate, picking their way with their flashlights. A sob escaped from Mother. Aunt reproached her for it. Then Mother began to cry a little louder. Without saying a word, Father walked ahead towards the house. Also walking towards the house supporting Mother, Aunt whispered repeatedly, "Please collect yourself. What will Mother do if you cry like this? Try to think of Mother, Mother!"

My mother stopped her own mouth with her fist. She thus managed to control her sobs when she stepped into the room.

Father, who had reached the room before any of us, was kneeling awkwardly before Maternal Grandmother, like one guilty, and was turning something over in his hand. It was the wet piece of paper that the village head must have handed over to him. Father was dripping water like just-hung laundry. But it was not only Father. All of us who had been outside, including myself, were making puddles on the floor with water dripping from our bodies. The thin summer clothes of Mother and Aunt were pasted to their skin, and revealed their bodies inside as if they were naked.

"I told you," Maternal Grandmother murmured again, as if to herself. "See?"

I had been watching Grandmother's moves for some time now with great uneasiness. I was paying more attention now to her working hands than to her incessantly moving sunken mouth. I noticed a change in the movement of her hands. It seemed that no one except me noticed the change. Even though she was preoccupied with her work with lowered eyes, as before, after we returned to the room from outside Grandmother's two gaunt arms were trembling slightly. Moreover, she was unconsciously dropping the fresh shelled peas into her lap that was filled with empty pods. I was afraid she would keep on making the mistake, and repeatedly looked out for a chance to give a hint to Grandmother, but each time I tried I found I could not open my mouth, so oppressive was the silence of the room. I could do nothing but watch her shaking, wrinkled fingertips even though I knew she would be dropping the empty pods good only for fuel into the bamboo basket that ought to collect shelled peas.

"Haven't I been telling you all along we'd have some tidings today, for sure?" Grandmother, whose hitherto pale face was momentarily flushed and looked ten years younger, murmured again. But as she broke the tip of another pod again and ran her finger through it, she instantly became ashen pale like a corpse, and aged ten years more in the selfsame posture. Grandmother was in a strange state of excitement. We could feel it from the way she breathed hard between words and the way she swallowed till her entire throat trembled.

"I knew several days in advance when your father died. I suppose you resented me, thinking this old woman mutters sinister words as a pastime, having nothing to do besides eat. But what do you say now? I'd like to know what you think of my premonitions. Do they still sound to you like the stupid words of an old woman? You mustn't think that of me, you mustn't. Even though I can't see and hear as well as you, I don't go around jabbering empty words. You're greatly mistaken if you think old women have nothing to do but waste precious food and murmur empty words. To this day my dreams have never predicted wrong. Whenever there was any calamity coming, my dreams have always predicted it."

Sitting erect at full height, with her head upright,

she reproached her daughters for not having acknowledged her prescience. Her face was again flushed red. What filled her bloodshot eyes as she looked at her daughters was akin to triumph. She seemed besieged with an irresistible desire to brag about the realization of her prophecy. As I gazed at her ridiculously triumphant expression, something like a spell hit me and my maternal grandmother suddenly looked to me like a weird, dreadful being. I could not help giving credence to her assertion that she had always, like an inspired prophet, unerringly predicted the approach of tragedy. Grandmother had gained her victory in the battle declared by herself, and she seemed still to have abundant energy left over after the battle to upbraid us for any imagined slight to her authority. To me, such an aspect of Grandmother gave a deep, ineradicable impression, as if she had been a being of inscrutable, unapproachable power.

Mother was raising her sobbing voice by imperceptible degrees. It began as thin as a thread, so that the other people in the room hardly perceived it at first. But as no one checked her, even when she had considerably raised her voice, she began at last to cry at full force. A mosquito had alighted on the nape of Aunt's bloodlessly pale neck and was sucking blood. But Aunt did not stir, sitting there like one out of her wits, even though the mosquito sucked until its belly was round and pink as a cherry. The door of the room was standing open. Even though mosquitoes swarmed in through the open door, nobody bothered to close it.

One could clearly guess at the progress of the people covered with military waterproof cloth by the shifting location of the dogs' barking. Receding from the moment the men left, the barking diminished further and further to the end of the village, and at last entirely died down. A black flying insect that had come in without my noticing it was disturbing the air of the room, flying around quite at its liberty. At last, after zooming through the room several times and almost putting out the lamp, it was caught in my hand. It was a mole-cricket. It writhed between my thumb and forefinger and tried to get loose. Thrusting out its strong forelegs which it used to dig up earth, it tried to break my grip. But what use were all its desperate struggles? Its life and death were completely at my mercy. I could kill it or let it live just as I liked. I began to put more and more pressure into my two fingers holding the insect. Just then I heard Grandmother murmur again.

"I'm not shaken. I knew all along this would happen. I'm all right."

Then, Mother's sobs reached their peak, and the whole room was filled with the painful, drawn-out lament that seemed to gnaw into our very bones.

"Poor Jun, poor Jun, what a fool you were to volunteer when others went into hiding to dodge conscription! Poor Jun, poor Jun, why didn't you listen to me when I told you not to become an officer? Now, what are we to do? What are we to do?" Her voice prolonged the words and trailed off into moans whenever the name of the dead man was pronounced.

The crimson-colored sobs of Mother, which filled the room in no time, soon spread into the yard steeped in the dark, and on the blanket of her sobs piled, layer upon layer, the shrieking rain of the long rainy season.

2

Gunjisan Mountain, which stood erect, piercing the sky with the tip of its peak, surrounded by a host of lesser mountains and hills, always looked dignified. There was a time, however, when this dignified Gunjisan Mountain took on a ridiculous aspect. For a time Gunjisan became a place where grown-ups gathered at night to play with fire. Sometimes we could see mist rising from the top of the mountain even in broad daylight. What an enormous amount of water must have been made on it by the grown-ups at night! Having experienced the bitter humiliation of making the round of the village wearing a rice winnowing basket over my head as punishment for bed-wetting, I could not help looking at the running brook in the village that started from the mountain with suspicious eyes. The rustic, taciturn and dignified mountain looked absurd, suddenly sending up smoke and fire. For grown-ups' play, it was childish and silly, but peaceful and tranquil. I had not then realized the relationship between the signal fire and the massacres. I could not have understood why, time after time, immediately after flames rose up from the mountain, there was a street battle in town and one of the villages was laid waste. But even had I understood such points, the result would have been the same. In spite of my ridiculous imaginings when first beholding the signal fire, Gunjisan Mountain shortly regained its dignified repose in my eyes and came to be even more dear to me.

One day, waking up, I found that thick black clouds had coiled around the mountain from the waist up. The rain had halted, but anyone could see from the dark cloud completely covering the eastern sky around Gunjisan that a bigger batch of rain than any we'd had yet was making preparations for an assault. From time to time, from the dark corner of the sky, lightning darted out and pierced Gunjisan as sharply as the bamboo lance that I once saw being thrust into a man's chest on the village road beside the dike. And each time thunder shook heaven and earth, like a scream sent out by the pierced mountain. I could very well imagine what the pain of being impaled by darting lightning must be like, and did not at all think the mountain cowardly for sending out such a miserable scream. It was clear that Gunjisan was being tortured by the sky from early morning.

I could tell Maternal Grandmother's approach even with my eyes closed. When she walked, there was no sound of footsteps but only the rustle of her skirt, so lightly and carefully did she walk, like a weightless person. Having approached so carefully, she emitted a strange smell. It was a very strange smell, such as one can sniff in the corners of an old, old chest, or an antique, or a deep pond of stagnant water. I vaguely felt the careful approach of my grandmother, who could be distinguished by a smell like that of ancient dust and the rustle of her skirt.

I was lying in the side room, pretending to be asleep. From the time I began to regard my grandmother as an awesome being, I had got into the habit of pretending to be asleep when she came near. Grandmother seemed to be taking twice her usual care so as not to awake her grandson from his nap. But I had already smelt my distasteful fill of that peculiar smell, and had already guessed what she was going to do. And I was not wrong, either. Maternal Grandmother's gaunt hand fumbled into my underpants. "Now let me feel my jewel," Grandmother would have said at other times. She would also have said, "This one's round as an apple, just like his maternal uncle's." But today, Grandmother did not say a word. She only silently moved her fingers, and felt my groin. This nameless act, which began from the time Mother's family came to live with us as refugees, was a big trial for me, and a very insulting experience. I'd dare anybody to claim I'm not telling the truth when I say I have never admitted my maternal grandmother's encroaching hand into my underpants without great displeasure. I don't know whether there may be any seven-year-old who would willingly consent to be treated like a baby; for my part, I had great pride in myself as a big boy with judgment as sound as any grown-up's, and such an act by Grandmother was a severe blow to my self-esteem. But there was no shaking her off, as I knew such a refusal would grieve her deeply, and there was nothing I could do but endure the insult.

As Grandmother's hand left my groin she gave a deep sigh. I could feel her gaze lingering on my face for a long time after her hand left my body.

"Poor thing!"

Leaving the two muttered words behind, she moved away. I opened my eyes a slit and peeped at Grandmother's back as she receded noiselessly, trailing her wrinkled cotton skirt. I don't know whom she may have meant in her lamentation just now. There were too many poor things around me. There was, of course, my maternal uncle who had just been killed in battle at the front. And, to speak the truth, I myself was also very much of a poor thing in those days. Since the incident of having accepted the bribe of a western sweet from a police detective, I had been cooped up inside the house for over a month now in penance, anxiously watching the moods of my father, who held command of housebound penance, and of Paternal Grandmother, in whose hand and in whose hand alone rested the power of forgiveness. But maybe the poorest thing of all was Maternal Grandmother herself. Maternal Grandmother, as she sat on the edge of the living-room floor, looked completely worn out. There was not a trace of the stubborn, awesome being glimpsed on the night we received the notification from the front. There simply sat a shabby, withered old woman gazing vacantly at the distant mountain. My joy at being freed from her unwelcome hand sank back to gloom at the sight of her pitiful figure.

For a few days after we learned of the death of my maternal uncle, the house was in chaos. Everyone was grieving, but my mother's grief was the most uncontrolled. Mother had her forehead tied with a white cloth strip as we children did on school sportsdays, and was quite bedridden with grief. She sat up from time to time to cry for a while, striking the floor with her palm amid loud lamentations, and then collapsed back on the bedding. At mealtimes, however, she sat up to eat hurriedly the bowl of barley Aunt brought in to her, and as soon as she finished eating she cried out with loud lamentations, thrusting away the meal tray, and sank back again on her bedding. Lying on her back, she would repeatedly mutter that her family ought to adopt a son and so continue the line.

Aunt's behavior was in sharp contrast to Mother's. From first to last, she did not show a drop of tears, nor did she exchange a word with anybody, nor did she eat a thing. Moreover, she silently took over all of Mother's work, and cooked, washed dishes, and did the laundry. Until I saw her flop backwards on the third day while trying to lift up a water pail beside the well in the backyard, I had been thinking that Aunt must surely be eating something secretly in the bamboo grove behind the house or in the dark kitchen. I had made myself easy on that point, thinking that Aunt, who had unbelievably strong will-power and sometimes completely confounded our expectations, would surely not go three days without eating a morsel.

But Mother and Aunt were not our greatest worry. What made us most uneasy was the discord between my paternal and maternal grandmothers. When my mother's family, which had moved to Seoul to give my uncle and aunt the benefit of education in the capital, suddenly appeared before us one day as refugees carrying bundles, it was my paternal grandmother who welcomed the family warmly and emptied the guest room for them to move in. We often heard my paternal grandmother express to her in-law counterpart her wish that the two old women could be each other's companion and support in the harsh times; and in fact the two old ladies got along perfectly well, without even a single discord, until that unfortunate day. They got along well even after the Republic's army recovered dominion over the South and my paternal uncle, who had till then been going around flourishing his arm-band as an officer of the People's Army, fled with the retreating communist forces, and my maternal uncle, who had till then kept in hiding in a dug-out cave in the bamboo grove, joined the Republic's army, and thus made each victory or defeat in the war a matter of conflicting emotion to the two old ladies.

The discord between the two old ladies began with that incident of my accepting the gift of a western sweet from a stranger, and thus earning the fury of Paternal Grandmother, who branded me a butcher of men who sold his uncle for a sweet, and therefore one not worthy to be treated as a human being. Maternal Grandmother earned the displeasure of her counterpart by protecting and defending me. The decisive rupture between the two grandmothers came on the day after we received the death notice of my maternal uncle. It was my maternal grandmother who made the provocation. On that afternoon also the weather was sinister, and forked lightning darted out of the clouds, repeatedly impaling the crown of Gunjisan Mountain. Maternal Grandmother, who had been watching the sky, standing on the edge of the living-room floor, suddenly began to utter dreadful curses.

"Pour on! Pour on! Pour on and sweep clean away all the red particles hiding between the rocks! Strike on, and burn to soot all the red particles clinging to the trees! Pour on, strike on! That's right! Thank you, God!"

All the family rushed into the living-room, but everyone was so stupefied that no one could say a word to check Grandmother's torrential curses. She continued to pour out vehement curses towards Gunjisan Mountain, which was said to be teeming with communist partisans, as if she could distinctly visualize red partisans being struck dead one after another by lightning.

"Has that old hag gone stark mad, or turned into a devil?"

The door of the inner room opened with a clatter and out came Paternal Grandmother, her face distorted with fury. I realised belatedly that there was a person in the house who could be Maternal Grandmother's match, and became tense.

"Whose house does she think this is, that she dares put on such horseplay?"

Maternal Grandmother looked around with vague eyes, like one awakened from sleepwalking by a violent shake.

"This is too good a spectacle for only a family audience, isn't it? I've heard of grace repaid with poison, and I'm seeing a case today. Fine coquetry this is, to one who gave you shelter from bombs! If you mean to go crazy, do so at least with a clean conscience. If you harbor such base ingratitude, lightning will fall on you!"

After thus subduing the other with imperious reproof, Paternal Grandmother continued her upbraiding:

"Do you think your curses will bring your dead son back and kill living people? Don't you imagine such a thing! Life and death are meted out by Heaven, and Heaven only. One lives as long as one's allotted to live by Heaven. And it is because of one's own sins that one has a child die before oneself. It's because of sins in an earlier life that a parent has to see a child die and endure the sorrow. It's your own fate that your son died. There's nobody to blame for it. You ought to know shame by now. Aren't you in your sixties?"

"All right. Granted it's because of my sins* that I lost my son. Is it because you're a blessed woman that you reared a son like that?"

"Listen to that! Hasn't she really gone raving mad? What do you mean, 'a son like that'? What's wrong with my son?"

"Think. You'll know if you're not a fool."

"Because you have no son left to offer you sacrifice after your death, you wish the same for everyone!"

"Stop it, both of you!" Father shouted.

"Wait and see. My Soon-chul isn't such a fool! You might not rest content until something happens to him, but Soon-chul can slip through showers without getting wet!"

"Stop it, please!" Father shouted again.

Mother had been pinching Maternal Grandmother's thigh all along.

"Did you hear what your mother-in-law said? She, who's an in-law relation, after all, calls me a woman without a son to offer sacrifices after her death. Isn't it misfortune enough to have given up an only son for the country, without being despised by an in-law? What mad words can a woman not utter, a woman who's lost a son? Does she have to reproach me thus for foolish words uttered in madness of grief, and

---

* This is not to be taken as the maternal grandmother's admission of having committed sins needing expiation. It is rather an announcement of her resolution to accept her suffering and sorrow in resignation. According to Buddhist theory of metempsychosis, one pays for one's sins in an after-existence, and thus there is no escaping the consequences of one's acts. This theory is often used by Koreans to "justify", and to reconcile themselves to, their unmerited sufferings for which there can be no explanation in terms of universal justice of reward and punishment. [Translator].

flaunt before me her possession of many sons? Answer me, if you have a mouth that can speak!''

Maternal Grandmother appealed to Mother, and Mother, with a tearful face, kept winking a pleading eye at Maternal Grandmother and pinching her leg. Paternal Grandmother, for her part, appealed to Father:

''Be careful how you judge, son! Is it wrong of me to rebuke an old woman who's praying for your brother's death? Must you, too, blame me? She may be your mother-in-law, but she's an enemy to me, and I can't live with her under the same roof! If you don't throw her out at once, I'm going to leave this house!''

''All right! I'm leaving! I spurn to live in this house any more! I'd rather die in the streets than stay a minute longer in a Communist's hou...''

Maternal Grandmother's hoarse voice stopped dead. She slowly turned her head and vacantly gazed at my father. Finishing the word ''house'' weakly and at length, she looked this time at Mother. Lastly, she gazed at me intently for quite a while, and shook her head left and right. Then she suddenly dropped her head. Her downward-bent gaze sank heavily towards a bamboo basket. Silently pulling the bamboo basket toward her knee, she picked up a pea-pod with a motion as silent as if she had been a shadow. Maternal Grandmother's face was as grey as a corpse's, and remained so from then on.

The turmoil created by Maternal Grandmother's words shook the whole house. When the word ''Communist'' came out of Maternal Grandmother's mouth, all the family members doubted their ears, and stood still in stupefaction. They could hardly breathe, and could only watch the slowly-moving hands of Maternal

Grandmother. "Communist" was a forbidden word among us, ever since we became a marked house in the village, watched by the police on account of my paternal uncle. This taboo was as strictly observed as the taboo against pickled shrimp juice during scrofula. Oh, to trespass such a solemn taboo! Maternal Grandmother's mistake was a fatal one, not to be pardoned by any apology, and the amazement of the family members was beyond description. But the one most amazed by the utterance was none other than she who uttered it. Maternal Grandmother did not offer any apologies. It was partly because all apologies were useless, but more because she tried to expiate her transgression by silently enduring all the censure of her in-law counterpart. No words can describe the fury of my paternal grandmother. She jumped up and down madly, foamed at the mouth, and almost fainted away. Then she tried to wrest an assurance from Father that he would expel Maternal Grandmother and Aunt from the house, and even Mother if she seemed sympathetic to them.

"You must drive them out this very day. And be sure to open their baggage before they step out of the gate. My silver hair-slide is missing, and it's not hard to guess who took it."

Aunt silently walked away to the guest room. After pouring out her fill of abuses, Paternal Grandmother lay down from exhaustion. The silence that ensued was soon shattered by the outburst of Mother's weeping. Instantly, Father's command fell like thunder.

"Shut up!"

Silence was a more unbearable torture than noisy unrest. Father strode out of the house. Maternal Grandmother remained on the living-room floor deep into the night, shelling peas with her gaunt, shaky hands. Father came back home only at dawn, dead drunk, reeking of sour alcohol.

Incandescent sparks of lightning kept piercing the crown of Gunjisan Mountain, thickly enfolded in black clouds. The signal fire which rose up almost every night from the mountain could not be seen any more since the rainy season began. Maternal Grandmother, who turned her eyes from time to time towards the mountain, looked pitifully lonely as she sat on the edge of the living-room floor. Maternal Grandmother said not a word today, even though lightning struck today just as on that other day. Ever since that unhappy quarrel with her in-law, Maternal Grandmother hardly opened her mouth. She kept moving her hands incessantly, the bamboo basket at her knee, as if shelling peas were the one and only task left for her in the world till her dying day.

3

A boy who had lately come to live in our village as a refugee from the north came to where we were playing, accompanied by a man wearing a straw hat. The boy, whose face was all scabby, said a few words to the man, pointing at me with his hand that had been scratching his bare, dirt-stained belly. The man gave me an attentive stare from beneath the wide brim of the straw hat which was shading a good part of his face. The boy from the north took what the strange man gave him from out of his pocket and sprinted away like a fleeing hare. The tall man with the straw hat walked up to me directly. His dark, tanned skin, his sharp, penetrating eyes, and his unhesitating stride were somehow overpowering to me.

"What a fine boy!"

The stranger's eyes seemed to narrow and, surprisingly, unlike what I expected from my first impression, a friendly smile filled his face. The man stroked my head a few times.

"You'd be a really lovely boy if you answered my questions straight."

The man's attitude made me extremely uneasy. I could not look into his eyes, so I opened and closed my hands for no reason, and kept standing there with my head lowered. In my palm was my paternal grandmother's silver hair-slide, which I had rubbed against a stone mortar into a giant nail, and which earned me victory over all the neighborhood boys in nail fights.

"Your father's name is Kim Soon-ku, isn't it?"

The man unbuttoned his white tieless shirt.

"Then Kim Soon-chul must be your uncle, isn't he?"

The man took off his straw hat. I had not said a word till then. But the man went on ingratiatingly. "That's right. You answer just like the clever boy you are!"

The man shook his straw hat as if it were a fan, holding open his tieless shirt to ventilate his body.

"I'm your uncle's friend. We're very close friends, but it's been a long time since we met last. I have something very important to discuss with your uncle. Will you tell me where he is?"

The man, whom I had met for the first time in my

life, used the standard Seoul dialect meticulously, like Aunt.

"Oh, isn't it hot! It's very hot here. Shall we go over there where it's breezy and talk a little?"

He forbade the other children to follow. When we reached the shade of a tree on the hill behind the village where other children couldn't see us, the man halted and fumbled in his pocket.

"I've got a very important message to convey to your uncle. If you tell me where he is, I'll give you these," the man said holding out in his palm five flat pieces of something wrapped in silver paper. He unwrapped one of them and proffered it in front of my nose.

"Have you ever tasted anything like this?"

The dark-brown colored thing gave off a delicious fragrance.

"These are chocolates. I'll give you all of them if only you answer my question straight."

I took a great deal of care not to let my eyes rest on the strange treat. But I could not suppress my swallowing.

"There's nothing to be shy about. It's natural for good boys to get rewards. Now, won't you tell me? If only you tell me what I've asked you, I'll be happy because you'll eat these delicious chocolates."

I don't know what it was that made me hesitate. Was it because I was undecided about the ethical propriety of accepting such a gift? Or was it because of the shyness of a country boy in front of a stranger, a shyness common to most country boys my age? I don't remember distinctly. But I think I remained standing there unresponsively for quite a while.

"Don't you want them?" the man pressed me. "You're sure you don't want them?" The man made an expression of regret. "Well then, there's no helping it. I did very much want to find you acting like a good boy and give you these delicious things. I myself don't need these sweets. Here, look. I'll just have to throw them away, even though that's not what I want to do with them."

Unbelievably, the man really threw one of them on the ground carelessly. He not only threw it down but stepped on it and crushed it. Casting a glance at me, he threw one more on the ground.

"I thought you were a bright boy. I'm really sorry."

He crushed the third one under his foot. There were only two pieces of the sweet remaining on his palm. It was evident that he was quite capable of crushing the remaining two into the ground. The man suddenly chuckled loudly.

"You're crying? Poor boy! Hey, lad, it's not too late now. Just you think carefully. Hasn't your uncle been to the house? When was it?"

It was at that moment that I felt I was powerless to fend off sophisticated grown-ups' tactics. Then, as I thought that this man might really be a friend of my uncle, my heart felt a good deal lighter.

The first few words were the most difficult to utter. Once I began, however, I related what had happened as smoothly as reeling yarn off a spool.

My paternal aunt who lived some eight miles off came to visit us, walking the entire distance under the broiling July sun. There was no reason for me to attach any special meaning to Aunt's visit, as she had several times come to our house without announcement to stay for a day or two even in those days of unrest. But things began to look very different when Mother, who had gone into the inner room with Aunt, sprang out of the room with a yellow complexion. Instead of sending me, as was usual, she ran out herself to fetch Father. Father, who had been weeding in the rice paddies, ran directly into the inner room with his muddy clothes and feet, without stopping to wash himself at the well. Mother, who returned hard upon his heels, fastened the twig gate shut even though it was broad daylight. Everybody seemed slightly out of their right senses. In the inner room the whole family, except Maternal Grandmother and Maternal Aunt and me, was gathered and seemed to be discussing something momentous. Around sunset, the three of us who had been left out were given a bowl of cold rice each. As I finished my meal, I saw Father had changed into clean clothes. I looked suspiciously at Father's back as he stepped out of the twig gate into the alley paved with darkness.

"You go to sleep early," Mother told me, as she spread my mattress right beside where Paternal Grandmother was sitting. It seemed that everyone was bent on pushing me into sleep, even though it was still early in the night.

"Wouldn't it be better to have him sleep in the other room?" Paternal Aunt queried of Mother, pointing her chin at me.

"I think it'll be all right," Paternal Grandmother said, "he sleeps deeply once he falls asleep."

"You must be dead tired from playing all day long. You must sleep like the dead until tomorrow morning, and not open your eyes a bit all through the night. You understand?'' Mother instructed me.

I knew that Father had not gone out for a friendly visit. It was obvious that he went out on important business. I wanted to stay wide awake until Father returned. I was determined to find out what the important business of grown-ups was that I was excluded from. To that end, it was necessary to pretend to obey the grown-ups' orders to go to sleep at once. I listened attentively for the least sound in the room, fighting back the sleep that overwhelmed me as soon as I lay down and closed my eyes. But no one said anything of any significance. And, before the important event of Father's arrival, I had fallen fast asleep.

I was awakened by a dull thud on the floor of the room.

''My God! Isn't that a bomb?''

I heard Paternal Grandmother's frightened voice. The two bulks that were blocking my sight were the seated figures of Father and Mother. Dull lamplight seeped dimly through the opening between them.

''Undo your waistband, too,'' Father said to someone imperiously. The person seemed to hesitate a little, but there came a rustle from beyond Father's bulk.

''*Two* pistols!''

''My God!'' Mother and Grandmother softly exclaimed simultaneously. Sleep had completely deserted me, and a chill slid down my spine like a snake. Even though I knew nobody was paying any attention to me, I realized it was unsafe to let grown-ups notice my wakefulness, and so I had to take painstaking care in moving my glance inch by inch.

I concentrated all my nerves on what was happening in the small space visible to me.

"Has Dongman gone to sleep without knowing I'm coming?"

As it seemed that Father was about to turn to me, I closed my eyes quickly. The shadow that had been shielding my face moved aside quickly, and lamplight pricked my eyelids.

"We kept him in the dark," Mother said proudly, as if that had been some meritorious deed.

"Don't worry. Once he falls asleep, a team of horses couldn't kick him awake," Grandmother insisted.

There was a short silence in the room. It seemed that nobody dared open his mouth. But my ears were brimming with the thick voice of the man who had sneaked into the house in the dark, carrying pistols and hand grenades. If that man is really my uncle, I thought, news of whom the whole family had been fretting about, his voice had, regrettably, become so rough as to be unrecognizable to me at first. His voice didn't use to be as rough as a clay pot that has been carelessly handled on pebbles, or so heavily gloomy that nothing seemed capable of cheering it up. As far as I could remember, my uncle chuckled heartily at the slightest joke, frown as his elders might on such manners, rarely remaining aloof from disputes, but always trying to involve others in them. He was easily excited or moved. But, no matter how I reckoned, there was no one but my uncle who could be the owner of that voice I had just heard. I imagined my uncle's face and form, which must have become as rough as the voice. Then, suddenly, I felt an uncontrollable itch in the hollows of my knees. The itch spread instantly over my entire body, as if I had been lying on ant-infested grass, and I had an irresistible yearning to scratch such parts as the middle of my back or my armpits or between my toes, places I could not reach with my hand to scratch while lying flat on my back without being noticed by the grown-ups. On top of it, my throat itched with an imminent cough, and my mouth filled with water.

Grandmother seemed most anxious to know what Uncle's life on the mountain was like. She heaped question upon question about how he fared on the mountain. To all the questions Uncle answered barely a word or two, and seemed irked by the necessity of saying even that much. But Grandmother seemed not to have noticed Uncle's mood, and kept on asking questions without end.

"You say there are many others besides you, but they must all be men. Who cooks rice and soup at each mealtime?"

"We do."

"You make preserves and season vegetables, too?"

"Yes."

"How on earth! If only I could be there beside you I'd prepare your food with proper seasoning!"

No response.

"Do they taste all right?"

"Yes."

"I know they couldn't, but I can't help asking all the same."

"They're all right."

"Don't you skip meals too often, because you move here and there?"

"No."

"Promise me you won't eat raw rice, however hungry you may get. You'd get diarrhoea. If you do, what could you do in the depths of the mountain? You can't call a doctor or concoct medicine. Do pay attention, won't you?"

"Don't worry."

"And since it's in the depths of the mountain, it must be cold as January at night, even in summer like this. Do each of you have a quilt to cover your middle at night?"

"Of course."

"Padded with cotton wool?"

No response.

"Don't stay in the cold too long. And, for frostbite, eggplant stems are the best remedy. You boil the stems and soak your hands and feet in the fluid. That takes out the frostbite at once. If I was beside you..."

"Please don't worry!"

"How can I help it? It tears my heart to see your frostbitten hands and feet. The times are rough, but for you, my darling last-born, to get so frostbitten!"

"Please, Mother, stop!" Uncle sighed with impatience.

"Do, Mother, that's enough," Father chimed in cautiously.

"Do you mean I shouldn't worry, even though my son's hands are frostbitten like that?" Grandmother raised her voice angrily. Such things were to her of the utmost importance. But Father also raised his voice.

"It's going to be daybreak soon, and you keep wasting time with idle questions! How can you worry about preserves and quilts when his life's at stake?"

Grandmother was silenced. Of course she had

many more questions, but a certain tone in Father's rebuke silenced her, stubborn as she was.

"What are you going to do from now on?" Father asked, after a pregnant silence. It was directed at Uncle.

"About what?"

"Are you going to go back to the mountain and stay there?"

When Uncle kept silent, Father asked him if he would consider giving himself up to the police. Father slowly began his persuasion, as if it was something he had carefully considered for a long time. Father emphasized again and again the misery of a hunted existence. Citing as an example a certain young man who had delivered himself up to the police and was now living quietly on his own farm, Father recommended urgently that Uncle do the same. He repeated again and again that otherwise Uncle would die a dog's death. A dog's death, a dog's death, a dog's death, a dog's death.

"Why do you keep saying it's a dog's death?" Uncle retorted sullenly. Uncle swore that before long the People's Army would win back the South. Vowing that he had only to remain alive until that day, he even recommended that Father should conduct himself so as not to get hurt when the government changed. Listening to his talk, I was struck once again by the great change in my uncle. His talk was fluent. In the old days, my uncle never used to be able to talk so logically. Because he had difficulty getting his points across by logical argument, he often used to resort to the aid of his fists in his sanguine impatience.

Uncle began to collect things, saying that he must go up the mountain before sunrise. It must have been

ing in multiple ranks in front of the gate. They were whispering things to each other and trying to look over the gate into the house. The wailing of women that I could hear from as far as the hill behind the village I now found to be coming from my house. As I approached all eyes turned on me. Villagers exchanged meaningful glances among themselves pointing their chins at me, and whispered again. The palisade of people suddenly parted in two, as if to make way. A strange man walked out ahead, and my father followed. One step behind him I could see the man with the straw hat. He was holding coiled around his hand the rope that bound both my father's hands behind his back. On seeing me, he grinned and winked. Father halted in front of me. His eyes seemed yearning to say something to me, but he silently resumed walking. At the gate Mother, Paternal Aunt and Paternal Grandmother were wailing and crying, repeatedly collapsing and sinking to the ground. Only then did pain begin to rise in me. During the entire day while I was ransacking the village in search of the boy from the north who had conducted the man with the straw hat to me, the pain assailed me sometimes with a sense of betrayal, or a terrible fury, or an unbearable sorrow that stung my eyes and stabbed my heart. The man with the straw hat had promised me on his oath that he would never tell anybody what I would tell him. It was the first mortal treachery I experienced at the hands of a grown-up.

From that night Maternal Grandmother became my sole protectress and friend. Between us there was the shared secret of sinners. It could have been that secret which gave the two of us the strength to support each other through many persecutions. My Paternal Grandmother was a woman of very strong temper. If she so much as caught sight of me, she started back as if she had stepped on a snake, and she refused not only to talk to me but even to let me have my meals in the inner room with the family.

Father returned home after spending seven full days at the police station. My mother, who made frequent trips to town to send in Father's food, sprinkled salt again and again on his head, sniffing and sobbing, as he stepped into the gate. Father's good-looking face had changed a great deal in those seven days. His eyes were sunken, his cheek bones stood out, and his face, which had become pale-bluish like newly bleached cotton, looked indescribably shabby. But what hurt me most of all was the look of pain that appeared on Father's face whenever he moved his right leg with a limping lurch. On the night of his return home, he ate no less than three cakes of raw bean curd which, along with the sprinkling of salt, was believed to be a good preventive against a second trip to the police station. Father had always been of taciturn disposition, but he uttered not a single word that day. From time to time he gazed vacantly at my face and seemed about to say something, but each time he withdrew his gaze silently. I was fully resolved never to run away should Father decide to give me a flogging, even if I were to die under his switch. And there, within his easy reach, were the wooden pillow and the lamp-pole. I felt I could not withdraw from Father's sight without receiving my due punishment. I waited, solemnly kneeling before him. But Father uttered not a word about what had passed. Only he did not forget to lay this command on me before lying down to sleep, "Dongman, if you ever so much as step an inch out of the gate from tomorrow I'll break your legs."

Ah, how happily I'd have closed my eyes for good, if Father had wielded his switch like mad that night, leaving these as my last words, "Father, I deserve to die."

4

The rainy front stayed on. The sky sometimes feigned benevolence by suspending the rain for a morning or an afternoon, but its frown did not relax at all; rather, the pressure of the iron-grey clouds increased, and malicious showers poured down fitfully, as if suddenly remembering. Everything between the earth and the sky was so saturated with wetness that if you pressed a fingertip on any wall or floor, water seeped out in response. All the world was a puddle and a slough. Because of the rain-soaked earth, the well water was no better than slops, and you could not drink a single drop of it without boiling it for a long time.

Even amid such persistent rain there was an attack by communist partisans under cover of night. Though there was a good five miles' distance between our village and the town, we could distinctly hear the noise of bullets like corn popping. Father, who had been up on the hill behind the village in spite of the rain, said that he could see a scarlet flame shooting up in the night sky even from that distance. The detailed news of the surprise attack spread through the village in less than a day.

One villager, who had been to town to ascertain

the safety of his brother's family, came by to see Father with our neighbor, Jinku's father, to give important advice. As soon as he sat down on the edge of the living-room floor, he gave a vociferous report of his survey in the town, not knowing that Paternal Grandmother was listening in the inner room beyond a paper-panelled door. He said that houses in the vicinity of the police station had suffered much damage, and that the red partisans who made the attack had been severely beaten. According to him, only a handful of partisans made the retreat to the mountains alive. What was most shocking in his report was his description of the corpses of partisans that he said lay scattered throughout the town. He described in vivid detail the hideous shapes of the corpses covered by straw mats. For example, he described one whose limbs were all torn apart. He said another had sixteen or seventeen bullet holes. The incident that attracted my interest was a corpse that the man said was thrown in the ditch folded quite double, with the back inside. I was greatly surprised that a man's body could be folded double, like a pocketknife, with the back inside. I couldn't believe that was possible. Lastly, he transmitted the news that the corpses were on display in the backyard of the police station, to be given to relatives or friends upon request. That was the point of his visit to Father. He recommended by hints that Father had better pay a prompt visit to the town police station. Jinku's father, who came with him, urged the same. Throughout their visit, Father had been wearing an expression of despair, and he showed great reluctance at the recommendation of the two men. But when the village head, who was Father's childhood friend, came by later and offered to accompany him to town, he resolved to do so at last.

Paternal Grandmother did not try at all to hide her contempt of Father for leaving for town in the rain, donning an oil-paper hat cover over his bamboo rain-hat. Paternal Grandmother had from the first opposed Father's trip to town. It was her conviction that the trip was entirely unnecessary. She even got furiously angry at her son, who still would not give credence to the decree of Heaven. What Grandmother maintained was simply this: whatever had happened in the town had nothing to do with Uncle; it was the providence of Heaven that Uncle would escape unharmed, no matter what danger he may have run into; Heaven had already appointed the date and even the hour that Uncle was to appear before Grandmother alive and entirely sound. Thus it was utter nonsense that Father should make the long trip to town to wade through corpses in search of such a brother. Grandmother, if no one else, had complete faith in this. Well, she not only had complete faith, but she had made detailed preparations against the happy event, and was waiting with outstretched neck. There was a reason for Grandmother's conviction. Grandmother's days, since the unfortunate flight of her younger son, had been a time of unbearable agony. She couldn't sleep, she couldn't eat, and she fretted all day long, waiting for news of her son. Then one day my paternal aunt, who had come to pay a visit, suggested that she consult a fortune-teller in the village next to hers. Thus, Grandmother made the trip to the fortune-teller, reputed to have divine prescience, carrying a weighty bundle of rice on her head as fee. Late in the evening, Grandmother returned home with a beaming face and summoned all the family to give highest praise to the blind man's foresight and to relate his oracle. Well, the ardently-awaited day, the day that was fated to bring our uncle home at a certain hour, was only a few days ahead of us now.

Father and the head of the village came back from town empty-handed. That Father's trip had been in vain as good as meant to us that Uncle would be returning alive. But it was strange that Father remained as taciturn as ever. There could be seen on Father's face two very different strands of emotion woven together. His face wore in rapid and irregular succession a look of relief, or a look of bleak despair. It seemed that Father, even if he could regard the absence of Uncle's corpse in the police station yard as meaning that Uncle was still alive, could not rest easy when he thought of the hardships and danger Uncle would have to endure in the future. But Grandmother was vexed by no such considerations. She became triumphant at once, and almost yelled that it was just as she had told us from the first, and that her son Soon-chul was not an ordinary human being. Then she fell to weeping aloud and, rubbing her palms together heatedly in fervent prayer, with her old worn-out face all muddled by continuously gushing tears, she made full, deep bows in all directions, in token of her gratitude to Heaven and Earth, to Buddha and the mountain spirits, ancestors and household gods. She looked like one gone mad, but her innocent faith and boundless maternal love moved the hearts of all of us. We all decided to believe. How could we have calmed her down without believing what she believed? It ended by every member of the family repeatedly reciting, solemnly and religiously, the date and the hour that my immortal uncle was destined to return to us, in repeated confirmation of our conviction. It was only after we realized that daybreak had stolen up to just outside the room that we went to bed, to have a preview of our happiness of that day in dreams. It was a long, long day that we lived that day.

Lying on my back in the guest room occupied by my maternal grandmother, I was dimly measuring the density of the rain outside the door by its dripping sound. The noise, which lifted and resumed and thickened and thinned, tickled my eardrums like the soft tip of a cotton swab. As I was still struggling with a heavy drowsiness on account of the fatigue from the night before, the noise of the rain sounded like a distant whisper in a land of dreams. Still under order of confinement at home, I sensed the long, tedious rain at times as a blessing. Had there been clear sunshine outside to make the fields and hills blaze with light, wind that shook the trees on the hills, and the cool chirping of cicadas, all the light and sounds of the world might have seemed like a curse to one who had to stay confined indoors without any amusement or distraction. On those occasional afternoons when the rain lifted a bit, I could hear very clearly, sitting in the room, packs of children noisily galloping through the village streets. Whenever I pictured the children gleefully drawing baskets of willow fish traps in the weedy pools around the river or in the forks of the irrigation ditches, and the silvery-scaled, plump carp they scooped up, I couldn't help sinking under the misery of a forlorn prisoner. I seemed to have already become a long-forgotten being among my contemporaries. My friends never stopped any more at my gate to call me out, even for appearances' sake. I therefore disconsolately picked up persimmon blossoms beaten down by the rain under the old persimmon tree beside the twig fence in the hours of envy when all the world seemed to belong to my friends, thus teaching myself resignation early in my life. The opening of school was all the hope that I had to cling to. The school, which had closed down because of the war, was to reopen soon, and then Father's order of confinement would lose effect, and my nightmarish house imprisonment would eventually end.

Maternal Grandmother stretched her back, pausing from shelling peas. Thanks to Grandmother, who kept silently moving her fingers all day long without ever saying a word to anybody, the major portion of the harvested peas had been sorted. But the pods that were still in storage in a corner of the barn showed signs of germinating. The moisture-saturated pods thrust up pale yellow sprouts. The task of shelling the peas before they became inedible fell to Maternal Grandmother. For some reason, all the family seemed to take it for granted that pea shelling was solely and entirely Maternal Grandmother's charge. And she herself seemed to take it for granted also, spending all her waking hours shelling the clammy things. Well, it may be more accurate to say that, because Maternal Grandmother regarded pea shelling as her appointed task, and jealously engaged in it lest someone should take the work away from her, all the others abstained from helping. At any rate, Maternal Grandmother, once

she sat down with a basket of pea-pods, kept quietly
moving her hands, seemingly oblivious to the passing
of time. From time to time she poured into the bamboo
basket her heavy sighs along with the round green peas.

Even though Maternal Grandmother's patience and
perseverance were truly extraordinary, sitting thus
immobile in one posture seemed to cause occasional
aches in her back. Thus, she now pushed the bamboo
basket aside and shook the lap of her skirt. She rubbed
her hands on her skirt and moved close to me. I smelt
the peculiar smell of Maternal Grandmother in the
lukewarm breath that descended on my forehead. I
guessed what was forthcoming. Sure enough, a chilly
hand that made my body shiver crept into my pants.
I had never, even once, felt pleased to lie thus under
Maternal Grandmother's gaunt hands.

"It's round as an apple, just like his maternal
uncle's."

I knew, without looking, that Maternal Aunt was
pulling her summer quilt up to her crown. Maternal
Aunt had been living for quite some days now almost
continuously lying on the warmer part of the floor
because something had evidently gone wrong with her
respiratory system. Aunt always pulled up her quilt like
that whenever Maternal Grandmother mentioned
Maternal Uncle.

"Who do you like better, your maternal uncle or
your paternal uncle?"

This was the unreasonable question Maternal
Grandmother had got into the habit of posing me. At
first I was extremely disconcerted when asked that
question. For one thing, it was a question meant for
extorting one answer. It was always Maternal Uncle

she mentioned first in the question. But my situation did not allow me to pick out either one as my favorite. If I were to tell the truth I would have had to say that I liked both of them. But Maternal Grandmother was demanding that I pick out one of the two.

"Do you like your maternal uncle, or your paternal uncle?"

But I knew that the important thing was neither the question nor my answer. I had long ago worked out that that question, posed without any emotion or stress, was simply an introductory remark to her long, rambling discourse. And so it was only the first couple of times that the question threw me into confusion. I thus lay there silently, pretending not to have heard the question. Then Grandmother would put on an expression of regret.

"I know. The arm always bends inward."

But it was only for a moment that the look of regret shaded her face. Her face regained equanimity soon enough, and she began her discourse.

"If you are really to be worthy of being Kwŏn Kil-jun's nephew you must first of all know what kind of a person he was. Unless you know what kind of a person your maternal uncle was, you're not fit to claim kinship with him. No, you're not."

The maternal uncle that my maternal grandmother described always wore a football player's uniform. And he dashed about like a thoroughbred mare on the infinitely vast playground rapidly constructed in my imagination. And he kicked the ball up sky-high, with a perfectly graceful motion. Maternal Uncle excelled in studies too, to be sure, but he was a genius in sports. And among sports, football was his speciality, and he was the leader of his school football team from middle school to college.

The first time Maternal Grandmother felt pride in her football-playing son was when she attended a football match for the first time in her life in the public stadium, when Maternal Uncle was in the sixth form. Maternal Grandmother, who had not wanted her only son to grow up to be a professional player, was dumbfounded when, after the game was over, hordes of schoolgirls rushed over to her and addressed her as "mother", as if she had been their mother-in-law. Even more amazingly, the girls praised her son to the skies, as if he had been their husband.

She was not one to brook such forwardness in nubile girls, and she chased them away after giving them a smart lecture, but the incident was not altogether displeasing to her. From then on, it became an important task for her to scold away with a stern lecture any schoolgirl fans who besieged her and her son.

"You should've seen your uncle that time...that time when the goalkeeper of the opposite team fell backward, struck by the ball your uncle had kicked. That'd have made it easier for you to answer — that you like your maternal uncle better than your paternal one."

Maternal Grandmother was not a woman of many words. But once she started talking of her son there was no stopping her. She was putting all her strength into her words, in an effort to implant deep into my heart the image of her splendid son. Sometimes she demanded that I describe my maternal uncle's features, as if afraid I might forget his face.

It is true that my maternal uncle was a splendid young man, worthy of any mother's pride. Even though there were some exaggerations and embellishments in Grandmother's memory, that he was an excellent football player and a much-admired figure are honest truths.

He was, in short, a brilliant and handsome man. His face was white as porcelain, and his sharp nose bridge and dark eyebrows gave him a truly distinguished look. His smiles, which revealed two neat rows of clean teeth, and his well-proportioned body gave him a look of refinement and good breeding. We had several times had him and his friends as guests for a few days. One time he came with quite a number of friends, all carrying rucksacks. The young men, who said they were on their way to Chirisan Mountain, played harmonicas and guitars all night long in the guest room. That night, one of his friends said he'd give me instructions on how to kiss girls, and rubbed his coarse jaw on mine and made me scream and flee from the room. That was when I was five years old. There was a time also when there was a beautiful young woman in the group. That was the year before the war broke out, and that time also he and his numerous friends carried on gleefully for five days, incurring the silent displeasure of my paternal grandmother, and putting Mother in an embarrassing position.

My maternal uncle's friends seemed to be treating him and the young woman like a royal couple. The group also locked themselves up in the room for hours at a stretch and seemed to be earnestly discussing something. Mother explained later on that they were in flight at the time, after a clash with leftist students with whom they were in long-standing opposition. Except for the period of about a month after the outbreak of the war, during which my maternal uncle was in hiding in the dug-out cave in the bamboo grove behind our house, these were about all the contacts I had had with him.

My feelings toward my uncle formed through such short contacts were closer to reverence than love as a kinsman. There were many things about him that could inspire my adoration. There was about his comely features and cultured manners and speech an almost feminine refinement; but his adroit movements and clear-cut decisiveness which had at its base his almost limitless energy bespoke manliness itself. The fact that he was a leader of an organisation at such an early age proved him to be a man of extraordinary qualities, and made him seem the more distinguished in my eyes. To me, the wondrous combination of such diverse abilities in one human being was an eternal enigma.

My paternal uncle was three years older than my maternal uncle. But, in spite of his seniority, he was much more youthful in his actions than my maternal uncle. His method of "rewarding" the labors of the supervisors of home-brewing and clandestine butchery who had earned the resentment of villagers for their harshness made him famous in the vicinity for a while. In the middle of a gathering of numerous villagers in the village square, my uncle gave each of the supervisors a large bucket of plain water to drink. He termed it their reward for their diligent labors in supervising clandestine brewing. Each of the supervisors had to gulp down the enormous amount of water, kneeling before the guns aimed at the napes of their necks. Then they were required to chant, marking time by striking their enormously swollen bellies, "I am the grandson of the yeast! I am the bairn of the cow! My father is an ox! A swine is my mother!" exactly one hundred times. Then they were asked to entertain the villagers with songs — any songs. Their hoarse singing, which sounded more like the bellowing of calves, sounded so miserable that the villagers who had been writhing with giggles all along stopped laughing in the end.

All his actions were comic and preposterous in such a way. There is also the famous anecdote of his "marriage" with the daughter of a small landowner in the neighboring village. With a notorious hoodlum of the village officiating, he "married" the daughter of Mr Choi in a sham ceremony. The ceremony also took place in the village square, and it was a completely modern, western-style ceremony, too. To it were invited, or summoned, Mr Choi and the bride's husband as guests. As soon as the ceremony was over, Uncle handed the bride over to the hoodlum who officiated and went directly up to Mr Choi. That day Mr Choi was beaten till he fainted away by the ruffian who kept calling him "father." That was in repayment for the atrocious thrashing he had received at the hands of Mr Choi's servants on the moonlit night he jumped over the wall of Mr Choi's house while drunk, after yearning for his daughter a long time.

My two uncles were thus antithetical. Whereas my paternal uncle's joining the red army was a blind and impulsive involvement in the whirlwind of events, just like his drunken jumping over Mr Choi's wall, my maternal uncle's activity in the right-wing movement and his volunteering for officership in the Republic's army were decisions grounded firmly on principle and made after careful weighing and examining of the meaning and consequences. Although they had not met often, my two uncles seemed to like each other well enough. If they hadn't, it would have been impossible for my maternal uncle to remain safe in hiding for over a month under the communist rule. Saying that it was only ignorant and poor men like himself who would wear red armbands, my paternal uncle treated my maternal uncle with respectful courtesy. It may have been an expression of envy and admiration for one who had received higher education than himself. At any rate, Paternal Uncle frequently bestowed kindly attentions on his in-law relation who had to stay in hiding in a cave. To Mother, he explained his kindly attentions by saying that it was in consideration of their mutual nephew, and the position of Father and Mother.

But my maternal uncle was different. Even though inwardly he felt warmly towards my paternal uncle, who was so cheerful and frank, outwardly he always cast cold glances at his counterpart who went around acting like a playful urchin. His intuition proved right. My paternal uncle, who seemed to have so much affection for my maternal uncle, dispatched his men to the cave in the bamboo grove on that mad dawn of the Communists' retreat. It was a few hours after Maternal Uncle, following a hearty supper, had silently disappeared without saying a word to anyone in the family.

I could hear Aunt coughing. Covered with the thin quilt up to her head, and lying still on her back on the warmer part of the floor, she was vomiting in coughs the pain that constricted her respiratory organs. I could hear Maternal Grandmother murmuring. And I could hear the noise of the thinning and thickening rain.

"He always disliked anything the least bit sloppy. I bet he died as neatly as he always lived. I'm sure only one bullet struck him, in the heart or in the head, so that he died instantly, without writhing or suffering pain."

It seems that Maternal Grandmother was severely shocked by what the villager recounted thoughtlessly the other day. It may be that the images of variously disfigured corpses went in and out of the guest quarter of our house all night long and disturbed the dreams of an unhappy old woman. It is certainly possible that they did. Maternal Grandmother was praying that her only son had met his death in battle in as neat and peaceful a posture as restful slumber. She prayed ardently that Satan's bullet had struck him in a vital spot, so that he crossed the boundary between this world and the next instantly, not only without bodily pain but also without feeling sorrow at leaving his old, widowed mother sonless in this sorry world. She murmured stubbornly that her son died with all the parts of his body intact, and that he could never have met the fate of those ghosts in ancient tales who had to linger in this world wandering over hills and plains in search of their scattered body parts.

But the voice was weakening perceptibly. Aunt's coughs, on the other hand, became more high-pitched. Grandmother's murmurs were becoming more and more subdued under the continuously invading noise of the rain.

5

The day appointed by the blind fortune-teller was inex-
orably approaching. The rain poured on, and everyone
was tired. With the exception of Paternal Grandmother, everyone was completely exhausted. Worn
out by waiting, and by the rain.

The stepping stones in the river that served as a
bridge between our village and the next had sunk under
the rising water long ago. After that, a thick rope had
been tied across the stream, so that grown-ups forded
the river against the rapid current coming up to the
waist by holding onto the rope, and children were carried across piggyback on the grown-ups' shoulders.
But, as the water was now deeper than a grown-up's
height, it had become utterly impossible to cross the
river. Thus, traffic to town had as good as closed down.
There were people who averred they saw things like
pigs, oxen and uprooted pine trees being washed down
the river from upstream, but Father brushed off such
rumors as nonsense. According to Father, our village
was located on the upstream shore of the Somjingang
River, so that such things could not happen unless there
was a great flood. But it was sure that this year's rainy
spell was unusually long and severe, and as a consequence traffic to and from the village was tied up,
which gave Paternal Grandmother grave worry.

"He's certain to be coming by the road from the
town. What a bother it is that the river's so swollen!"

There was a toad that had taken up abode in the
dirt verandah of our house for many days, despite my
manifold persecutions. It seemed to deem itself lucky

to have found a shelter at all after having its cave wrecked by the long rain. Pitiable as it was, it aroused my mischievousness by the absurd sight it presented as it dragged its clumsy body around under the wooden floor or on the dirt verandah. On the third day, I turned it bellyside up and, inserting a barley straw in its anus, blew into the straw until its belly was puffed up like a rubber ball. After that it disappeared for an afternoon. But the next morning it was back on the dirt verandah, claiming its right of residence. Squatting on the stepping stone, it gazed vacantly with its protruding eyes at the water dripping from the eaves.

On one of those days, trouble was discovered in the barn. It was not the kind of trouble that broke out suddenly one morning, but rather a gradual development over many days, but because no one had noticed it we were all aghast at the discovery. A mist began rising from the bags of barley that had been stored in the barn as soon as they were reaped. As the peas had done some time ago, the grain was now sending up pale yellow sprouts. It was lucky that Father made the discovery when he went in to set mousetraps; otherwise, all the family would have simply had to starve until harvest in the autumn. Suddenly the entire family went around busily, as in the peak farming season. To store the barley bags so as to prevent further damage was a big problem. We installed a storage platform of wooden bars in the barn to provide ventilation space between the floor and the barley bags, and spread the steaming barley on all the level places in the house to let it dry. Wherever I went — bedrooms, kitchen, everywhere — there was barley. I detested barley, and not only because it felt rough in the mouth and gave tummy aches. Whenever I saw the slit in the barley grain I recalled a legend told me by Paternal Grandmother.

Once upon a time there lived a boy whose father was ill with a fatal disease. The boy consulted a doctor, who prescribed a concoction made out of live people's livers. The boy therefore killed three people he met on his way home — a scholar, a monk and a madman — and made a broth with their livers, upon drinking which the father's disease was entirely cured. The boy buried the corpses in a sunny place. The next year, a strange plant was seen growing on the tomb, and its grain was what we now call barley. The slit in the barley grain is thus the slit the boy made in the bodies of the men for the purpose of taking out their livers.

It was truly uncomfortable inside the house with its floors covered all over by such an unpleasant grain. I felt cornered and bound. But Paternal Grandmother was a woman of truly amazing determination. Even in the midst of the fuss, she simply went on with her plans. First, she ordered Mother to take out of the chest her treasured silk cloth and sew a Korean-style outfit for Uncle. In her opinion a Korean suit is the most dignified and comfortable garment for indoors. And she made Mother prepare Uncle's favorite dish — fried squash slices — in mountainous heaps, despite Mother's protest that it would get spoiled and become inedible in two days. She seasoned the fern fronds herself, and complained that because the times were hard, plants didn't grow as they ought to. All the dishes that were liable to become spoiled were heavily salted or deep fried to prevent deterioration. At last the preparations were almost complete. There was food enough to give an ordinary village-scale feast for country people like us. Grandmother's face, as she looked around the kitchen, lit up with the pride of one who has accomplished an important task. Now there was only one worry still left for her.

"He's sure to be coming by the road from town. What a bother it is that the river's so swollen!"

"What's there to worry about in that? Even if the river's swollen a bit, how could it hinder his coming, if he's destined to come? He knows traffic often gets tied up in the rainy season, so he'll take the stone bridge and come by the circular road."

Father brushed aside Grandmother's worry, to put her at ease, but Grandmother shook her head.

"Of course he'll take the circular road. But that's four miles longer. Four miles sounds pretty short, but think of walking four more miles in this rain. And his feet frostbitten, too!"

Paternal Aunt came the day before the appointed day. As soon as she arrived she inspected the cupboards and shelves in the kitchen, and complimented Mother and Paternal Grandmother for their thoroughness. She seemed quite satisfied with the preparations that had been made. Aunt showed as complete a faith in the homecoming of my uncle as had Paternal Grandmother. It was this aunt who had introduced Grandmother to the blind fortune-teller. As she was thus the one who induced my grandmother's complete faith in the fortune-teller, it was understandable that she held as firm a belief in Uncle's homecoming as did Grandmother. But her idea of a fit welcome for the returning uncle was so perfectly identical with Paternal Grandmother's that even my mother, who was chary

of complaints against her in-laws, marvelled secretly
to Maternal Grandmother and Maternal Aunt on the
resemblance of taste between her mother- and sister-
in-law. It was not as if Mother was not hoping for
Uncle's return. Even Maternal Aunt, who hardly ever
spoke in those days, and Maternal Grandmother, who
had once invoked curses upon communist partisans,
silently wished for the happy reunion of the relations
as they watched the heated preparations. But wishing
and believing are two different things. I also ardently
wished for my uncle's return. But even in my childish
judgment it did not seem very likely that an event like
that could occur as easily as predicted. If Uncle were
to come, in what status and by which road would he
be coming?

I had chanced to overhear Father talking to Mother
in the kitchen. Father said that such a thing was
impossible. If one detached oneself even a little from
Paternal Grandmother's touching faith — and it was
a complete, unshakable faith — and examined the matter with any objectivity at all, the impossibility of the
prediction being fulfilled was so evident that it made
our hearts ache. As a last resort, Father thought of the
possibility of Uncle's having surrendered himself to the
police somewhere, but he quickly denied the likelihood
himself. Had that been the case, we would have had
by now some notice of interrogation from the police.
Father knew better than anybody else that our family
was under surveillance. There was a man who could
be seen sauntering up and down along our twig fence
at times and casting suspicious glances into the house.
Though outwardly we had freedom of movement, we
were like fish securely cooped inside the net drawn

by that man. I knew from long before that the man sometimes dropped in at our neighbor Jinku's to gather information about what was going on in my house, and that once or twice he even called my father out to a tavern for a talk.

It was I who shuddered most of all when the man came into view. His appearance had dreadful meaning for me. It always awakened anew my guilty conscience, which I was trying to lull to sleep. The sight of him always made me recall Paternal Grandmother's voice as she called me a butcher of men who sold his uncle for a sweet. Father should have struck me dead that night with the wooden pillow. It gave me unendurable pain to behold Father's face as he returned from a talk with that man.

The only way I had of escaping from my paternal grandmother's censure that kept reviving in my memory was to imagine myself dying in the most pitiful shape. That was the only way of comforting myself out of the tormenting consciousness of guilt. I pictured to myself the scene in which the whole family, especially my paternal grandmother, shed tears without end in front of the dead youth. The greater Paternal Grandmother's sorrow and regret, the more sweetly consoling it was to me. But when I woke up from the daydream I always found myself as impudently alive as ever, and I could not but dread meeting Paternal Uncle face to face. It was because of this guilt that, while ardently wishing for my uncle's return, I also secretly harbored the horrible wish that I might never have to face Uncle again — that Uncle had died long ago in some steep, deserted valley and would never be discovered by anybody. Really, the anticipated day, which was just one day ahead now, filled me with mortal dread. I was so terrified that I prayed today would never end.

But I think my terror and anxiety were nothing compared with the pain my father endured. I had heard Father pleading in the kitchen with Mother, who was complaining about Paternal Grandmother's excessive vigilance.

"I feel the same as you do. It's a hundred to one that he won't come. And even if he does by some extraordinary chance, it won't be an event of the kind Mother plans it to be. That I know better than you do. But what can I say to Mother? It's best simply to do everything that she bids us. That's better than making her think we're trying to thwart her joy and giving her a grievance. Don't you think so?"

Father was appealing to Mother by telling her of his own agony at having to follow his old mother's lead, even having to seem assiduous in following it, while knowing the waited-for event to be an impossibility. Even though Paternal Grandmother's faith, nourished by her boundless motherly love, moved our hearts at first and made us pray for the fulfilment of her expectation, we were far from having the same faith ourselves. We were only hoping and waiting with her because we did not want to disappoint the old lady on any account. Father had already foreseen the despair that would follow Grandmother's disappointed expectations, and the terrible aftermath of that despair. But there was nothing any of us could do except try our best not to cross the old lady. It was a pity that the blind fortune-teller, reputed to be divinely inspired, had not told Grandmother which road Uncle would be taking for his homecoming.

It was already night. The rain, which thinned down from around dusk, was now a mere misty drizzle. Into the hazy halo of the lamp hung on the gatepost the rain descended in sprinkles of powdery drops, as if it, too, was quite exhausted. Even though ever since the beginning of the war the whole village was in the habit of extinguishing all light after supper-time, without any express order, we had hung out a lamp tonight, letting it keep vigil through the night like a lonely sentinel. It was, of course, at Paternal Grand-mother's insistence. Who knows, she said, even though Uncle was due to arrive from around eight to ten o'clock tomorrow morning, he might be coming in the middle of the night due to some sudden change of plan. Grandmother did not want it to look as if the family was unprepared for his return.

"It was for an occasion like this that we saved up the expensive kerosene."

She ordered one more lamp to be hung from the eaves and warned us not to let the lamps die out in any of the rooms. She explained very succinctly the reason we had to keep the house as bright as day.

"We have to keep the lamps burning bright so he can spot the house from far, far away and run all the way home, knowing his mother's waiting for him with wide-open eyes all through the night."

The night deepened. Even so, nobody seemed to be thinking of going to bed. No one in the family had the guts to spread out bedding when Paternal Grand-mother was tensely surveying the house all over. The weather also seemed to be flattering my grandmother. The long, fierce rain had changed to a drizzle in the evening, and then by degrees withdrew out of sight and out of hearing, so that as the night deepened even the dripping from the eaves ceased. And the cool wind that carries away humidity began to blow. Well, the rainy spell had persisted long enough, and it was time for the rain front to retreat. But Grandmother quickly related the change in the weather to the forthcoming happy event of the morrow, to her great satisfaction.

It must have been long past midnight. I had left the inner room to come to the guest room and lie down beside Maternal Grandmother. Neither my maternal aunt nor my maternal grandmother was asleep. With all the tense excitement in the inner quarters they couldn't fall asleep, I suppose. Aunt was lying still on her back, facing the ceiling, and Grandmother was seated leaning on the wall, facing the door. My eyes were tracing the flickering shadow of the lamp's sooty flame on the ceiling. My ears were wide open, and were listening to the songs of the night in the distant grass beyond the darkness outside the door.

All around was quiet. The house couldn't be quieter, even had everyone been asleep. It was so perfectly still that the stillness rather hampered my listening to the sound of darkness. It was as if my auditory organs were being paralysed under the pressure of the stillness that weighed all around. So much so that I sometimes suspected that the sounds that came to my ears were not sounds that actually existed in the world but rather some illusion created by my bewitched brain. But collecting myself and listening again, I seemed to be hearing some wakeful being besides myself patiently filing away in the darkness at the edge of the vast stillness with a sharp file. For a long time I had been concentrating on distinguishing amid the whisper of the wind the chirp of the crickets from the chirp of the katydids, and was relishing the sweet and sour tastes of the sounds. Suddenly, there sank into the midst of the murmur of insects an unfamiliar sound, and its strangeness made me tense. But the sound ceased as unexpectedly as it began. As it fled, just as I was about to grasp the tail end of it, I felt again darkly that I might have been bewitched by something. But the sound came again after a pause. It was very distinct this time. It was not loud, but it was distinctive among the many hushed sounds of the night. It was like the sound made when children blow into the mouth of an empty bottle or like the siren of a ship on a distant sea. It was, at any rate, a faint but pregnant sound. It was also a very obscure sound, and I was completely at a loss to discern its direction. It seemed now to be coming from somewhere around the river's shore outside the village, or from the kitchen garden of our house, right outside the door. The strange, secretive sound that stole through the stillness of the night — I lay bewitched by it. Like a boy chasing fox-fire in the graveyard, my consciousness was already rushing to the river's shore, drawn by the mysterious strain of the eerie sound.

"It's the whisper of the king snake," Maternal Grandmother said. Her words, which fell upon me like a huge, dark shadow, almost made me scream.

"It's the king snake calling up the snakes."

Grandmother's words coiled round my body like a huge snake darting out its forked tongue, and I could hardly breathe. It was my beloved maternal aunt who chased away the chilly feel of the snake against my body. I had a protector. I was infinitely thankful that I was not the only one to have heard the sound. My aunt was already sitting up beside me and staring at the door. Maternal Grandmother twitched her lips, preparatory to saying something more. Aunt put her hand on my shoulder and gave Grandmother a sideways stare.

"Don't!"

But Grandmother kept twitching her lips. Had not Aunt subdued her once more, Grandmother would surely have said something.

"Please don't!"

Aunt pulled me under her quilt. Buried snugly under Aunt's armpit, I heard the sound once more. The sound like a ship's siren from a distant sea once more scattered chill all over the room. This time, too, it was indistinguishable whether the sound was coming from the river's shore or from the kitchen garden of our house. Then there was a long interval. The snake's call sounded for the third time, and then came no more. But the aftertaste of the sound lingered in the room for a long time and kept our mouths shut. Maternal Grandmother was still sitting in an awkward posture, stooping forward toward the door. Waves of emotion crossed her face. Sometimes she looked vacantly into space, like a person hit hard on the head, but the next moment she looked out beyond the door with narrowed eyes, like someone trying to work out a very complicated problem. At last she turned towards me and Aunt.

"Dongman," she called. "Dongman, my dear."

But when my eyes met hers she averted her face. After some hesitation, she slowly opened her mouth.

"Do you think so, too?" she asked, apropos of nothing, and again hesitated for a long while.

"Do you also think that what happened to your uncle happened because of me?"

I decided to answer the question. The voice asking the question was so urgent that I thought I had to say something in response. But I realized the next moment that no answer was necessary. She was not looking at me, nor was she paying any attention to me. She was completely absorbed in her own thoughts. She would not have heard me even if I had said anything in response.

"No! What happened that night was none of my willing. I'd no thought of spying on anybody. I'd been to the outhouse and saw the light in the inner room and heard whispering voices, so I just went nearer to see what was going on. Who'd have known it'd bring about such consequences? A team of horses couldn't have led me there if I'd known such a thing was going to happen. I'm not saying I did well to be so curious. I know I shouldn't have done it, but it's wrong to think it's because of me that things ended that way. Even if it hadn't been for me, your uncle would've returned to where he came from, as he was fated to do. That was his lot."

Aunt hugged me tightly. With my face buried snugly between Aunt's breasts, I heard Grandmother's murmurs in dreamy cosiness. Then, my whole body loosened up as after a heavy flogging and violent weeping, and drowsiness utterly overwhelmed me. Even in my dreamy exhaustion I vowed to myself that I would marry my aunt for sure when I grew up, and my ears grew inattentive to Grandmother's murmurings.

6

I woke up, before I was sufficiently refreshed, to the sound of Paternal Grandmother's furious reproaches uttered just inside the gate. Although the sky was brightening, it was still early dawn. Summer nights are short, and, as I had gone to sleep long past midnight, to wake up in early dawn meant I had as good as skipped sleeping that night. I felt a numbing pain inside my head, and my eyelids kept sliding down. But my condition was vigor itself compared with the rest of the family's. Because of many days' fatigue and tension, Father's face was swollen and yellow as in jaundice, and Mother had become gaunt as a mummy. Maternal Grandmother and Maternal Aunt were not much better. But Paternal Grandmother was energetically imperious, loudly scolding the wearied family from early dawn. She was giving an awesome bawling-out to Mother and Father.

The lamp hung on the gatepost had died out. The wind must have blown out the flame — the oil can was more than half full, and the glass shade was wet with drops of water. The blown-out lamp had infuriated Paternal Grandmother. She took it as a test God had put on Father's and Mother's devotion. Grandmother's ire was not soothed by giving Father and Mother a severe scolding. She declared that this proved to her that Father and Mother were not fit to be trusted with looking after Uncle's welfare, and announced her resolution to take charge of the keys to the barn and the safety cabinet until she saw signs of amendment.

"I won't say anything more this morning, because

a woman shouldn't raise her voice on the morning of festivity. I'll leave the rest up to you. I won't move a finger, but just entertain myself with watching what you do." Then she clicked her tongue in self-pity as she turned around to head for the inner quarters. "Lucky woman I am, to have such a thoughtful elder son!" She strode across the yard toward the inner room. "What sins am I expiating, to be blessed with a son and a daughter-in-law such as those?" she grumbled to herself as she passed in front of the guest room, loud enough to be heard by neighbors.

Paternal Grandmother was as good as her word. She really did not move a finger. After she went into her room, slamming the door shut, she did not utter a single comment on what was going on outside. Instead, she kept a keen watch over what was happening in the yard through the glass pane of the small window, and did not remove from her face a disapproving, discontented look. All of us in the family came out with brooms or other utensils and, with a keen consciousness of supervisory eyes upon us, swept the yard, scrubbed the floor, cleaned cobwebs, and tidied the house. Paternal Aunt and Maternal Aunt also joined in, and the house regained the neat appearance it had had before the long rain. Maternal Aunt and Paternal Aunt went into the kitchen with Mother to help with the breakfast, and Father and I dug a deep ditch between the footpath leading from the gate to the yard and the kitchen garden, sweating profusely, to drain the water from the yard.

The sky was still cloudy. We had hoped to see the sun for the first time in a long while, but the sky did not look cheerfully disposed. Nevertheless, a corner of the western sky was clear, and there was a cool wind that drove away the clouds. There was no sign anywhere of a renewal of rain. Even that much beneficence was a blessing to us. Not only my family but everybody felt the same. Village people who dropped in on us from early morning began their greetings by talking of the weather. Then they talked of Uncle. The men accosted Father very smoothly, beginning with comments on the weather, and the women kept going in and out of the kitchen. My house overflowed with village people, as on a feast day, and the members of the family were kept busy responding to inquisitive neighbors. What the neighbors were most curious about was to what extent the members of our family believed in the prophecy. Of course they did not use words like "superstition." Although they expressed wonder at the fact that one word of a fortune-teller could lead to such large-scale preparations, they were polite enough not to treat it as mere foolishness, at least in our hearing. They tended rather to be sympathetic, and commented encouragingly that the devotion of the family, if nothing else, would bring back Uncle. Father simply smiled. Father saw, in the attitude of some of the people who spoke thus, that they were amusing themselves with what was going on in our house. Some of them were taking exactly the tone of the doctor who tells his dying patient he'll be well in a few days. As it drew near the appointed hour, more and more people gathered at the house, so that our yard teemed as on a village festival day. It looked as if everyone in the village who could walk on his own legs had drifted there. I could see the stranger smoking a cigarette, sitting on the porch of Jinku's house. My house was bustling like a marketplace, and the family had still not had breakfast. Grandmother had forbidden us to eat, as all of us were to eat together when Uncle came. It wasn't as if we were starving, so I resolved to be patient, but my stomach howled very pitifully.

At last it was eight o'clock, the beginning of the period* appointed by the fortune-teller. Time raced past, amid the tense excitement of everyone. Soon it was nine o'clock, and then it was approaching ten o'clock. But the long-awaited Uncle did not show up.

After the villagers had all dispersed we sat down to a late, late breakfast. Only the village head and Jinku's family remained to try to console us. Paternal Grandmother remained in the inner room, and the rest of the family sat around the table set in the side room. The spoons moved slowly, although the table was luxuriously laden with colorful dishes. Paternal Grandmother refused to eat breakfast, even though she told the family to go ahead and eat. Her spirit was not sunken, even though the time appointed by the blind seer was quite past and gone. Well, she still *looked* spirited, anyway. She said that from the first she had not thought the hour was all that important. What was important, according to her, was the day, not the hour. She said that there could be accidental errors even in events supervised by Heaven; and man often cannot move exactly to schedule. She insisted one must make allowances for slight errors even in the prophecy of divine seers. For Grandmother, the day was still only just begun. She said that, since he could not fail to come

* The fortune-teller had predicted that the uncle would return in *Chinsi*, the hour of the dragon, which is from eight to ten o'clock in the morning. [Translator].

that day, she would wait a little longer and have her first meal of the day with her son. She did not betray any tiredness.

Our dog Wolly, who had been peering in at the rooms, standing with his forefeet on the edge of the living-room floor and smacking his lips, suddenly stepped down to the dirt verandah. We heard Wolly bark, turning to the gate. Then we heard a shout of children. Father's spoon stopped still in the air, and all of us instantly ceased all movement. Children's exclamations were rapidly approaching our house. Flinging the spoon away, I ran outside. The noise instantly surrounded our gate. I was hit by the shouts of the children in the middle of the yard. The first thing that came into my view was a pack of children with gaping mouths. All of them had rocks or sticks of wood in their hands. The children hesitated a little before the gate, not daring to rush into the house, and raised their weapons threateningly. One of the boys threw his rock forcibly. Where the rock fell I beheld the thing.

There was a lengthy object sliding into the house. It was a huge snake, longer than a man's height. My whole body constricted the moment I saw its horrible bulk with its yellowish scales glittering dazzlingly as it slid, reviving in my memory the eerie whisper of the night before. But I was a boy, and a snake meant an adventure. Horror had a moment's grip on me, but the next moment I was as excited as any of the other boys who kept screaming and throwing rocks. I could not control the aggressive, destructive urge that male children instinctively feel towards all reptiles. I ran over to the barn and fetched the big wooden staff that Father used when carrying heavy things on a pannier.

I raised both hands high in the air, ready to strike the snake dead if it moved an inch nearer me, but a hand grabbed my arm with rough force. I looked around to see that it was Maternal Grandmother. At the same moment, there arose a piercing scream from behind me.

"Aaaack!"

With that, Paternal Grandmother fell on the floor as limply as a piece of worn-out clothing. Maternal Grandmother twisted the staff from my grasp. Her eyes glared at me in silent reprimand.

The unexpected appearance of the huge snake threw the whole house into utter confusion. The most urgent problem was Paternal Grandmother, who had fainted. The family gathered in the inner room to massage her limbs and spray cold water on her face in an effort to bring her around. The village people, who had dispersed, gathered in the house once more, and talked and exclaimed so noisily that it was like sitting in the middle of a whirlwind. It was only Maternal Grandmother who did not lose her calm in the midst of the noise and confusion. As if she were simply carrying out prescheduled procedures, she put things in order one by one with a truly amazing composure. First of all, she drove away the people. With the help of the village head and Jinku's father, she drove out all the village people who came for the show, and locked the gates fast. The children and grown-ups who had been driven out of the gates came round to the part of the twig fence next to which stood a persimmon tree. The huge snake, taking advantage of the heated confusion, had slid down the kitchen garden through the grown mallows and lettuces, and had already coiled itself around the upper branches of the persimmon tree. Its yellow body wound around the persimmon bough, it kept darting its wiry tongue in and out. It must have suffered a deadly blow, for its tail was more than half cut from the body and dangled precariously. The tireless children had followed it up to the persimmon tree and were still throwing rocks and sticks.

"Who's that throwing rocks?"

Maternal Grandmother's reprimand was sharp as a sword.* All throwing ceased. Then Maternal Grandmother began slowly walking to the persimmon tree. Nothing happened even when Maternal Grandmother stood upright just below the persimmon tree with the coiled snake, and sighs of relief escaped from the people who had been watching with breathless suspense. Maternal Grandmother did not waver a bit, even though the snake's fiery dots of eyes gleamed in all directions and it raised and lowered its head threateningly. Grandmother slowly lifted both hands and clasped them palm-to-palm on her bosom.

"My poor boy, have you come all this way to see how things are doing in the house?" Grandmother whispered quietly, in the tone of one singing a lullaby to a fretful baby. Somebody giggled. Instantly, Grandmother's eyes grew sharply triangular.

"What mongrel is it sniggering there. Come up here at once! I'll wring your neck!"

Everybody hushed still as death at Grandmother's fiery rebuke. Grandmother turned to the snake again.

---

* The giant, venomless snake was believed to have supernatural properties and powers. It was believed that spirits of the dead could enter it to visit people in this world. It behoved people, therefore, not to hurt it but to conciliate it by all means. [Translator].

"As you can see, your mother's still in good health and everybody's doing all right. So put your mind at ease and make haste on your own way."

The snake did not stir a muscle. It only darted its wiry tongue in and out, and raised its head a couple of times.

"You mustn't linger here crouching like this any more when you have such a long way to go. You shouldn't, you know, if you don't want to grieve your family over-much. I know how you feel, but you must consider others' feelings, too. What would your mother feel if she knew you were lingering here like this?"

Maternal Grandmother was earnestly entreating, as if the snake had been a real live human being. But, however ardently she pleaded, the snake did not show any inclination to move away. A neighborhood woman then told Grandmother the method for expelling snakes. The woman, whose body was hidden from view and whose voice only could be heard, said that you could chase away snakes with the smell of burning hair. At Maternal Grandmother's bidding I hurried into the inner room to get some of Paternal Grandmother's hair.

Paternal Grandmother was lying under a quilt, stiff as a corpse. Although she was breathing, she was still unconscious. I urgently demanded some of Paternal Grandmother's hair from the family members sitting around the unconscious form with ashen-grey faces, waiting for the arrival of the doctor. My demand must have sounded preposterous. It took quite a long time to explain what use Grandmother's hair would be. It took a longer while for Paternal Aunt to collect a handful of Paternal Grandmother's hair by combing the unconscious old lady's hair with a fine-toothed bamboo comb. The hair collected from repeated combing was given to me at last. When I came out to the yard, Maternal Grandmother had in the meanwhile prepared a small tray of a few dishes. On the round tray were Uncle's favourite dishes of fried squash slices and seasoned fern, and there was also a large bowl full of cold water. After taking the knot of hair from me and putting it on the ground, Maternal Grandmother slowly raised her head and looked up at the persimmon tree.

"These are what your mother has prepared for you for many days. Even though you can't taste them, take a good look at them at least. They're all proofs of your mother's devotion. It's not that I'm trying to get rid of you. You must understand that. Please don't blame me too much for the bad smell. It's just to hurry you along on the long way you have to go. Put your worries at rest about your family, and just take good care of yourself on the long way ahead of you."

As she finished talking, she turned up the live coal in the tinder bowl. When she placed the knot of hair on it, it burned with a sizzling sound. The smell of burning protein quickly spread all around. What happened next drew an exclamation of astonishment from everyone. The huge snake, which had till then been immobile as a rock despite all Grandmother's entreaties, slowly began to move. It's body, which had been coiled round and round the persimmon tree, smoothly unwound itself and the snake dropped to the ground. After hesitating a little, the snake slowly and waveringly crept towards Grandmother. Grandmother stepped aside to make way. She followed its tail as it slid away and kept chasing it, making a swishing sound with her lips. Like chasing away sparrows from the fields, Grandmother swished and even clapped her hands. The snake crawled over the ground noiselessly, twitching its gleaming scales. All the members of the family also spilled out to the living-room floor and fearfully watched the snake sliding across the yard. Wolly, whose tail clung to his inner thighs, dutifully barked with a fear-strained voice from beneath the living-room floor. The snake slowly coursed its way through the empty space between the barn and the kitchen, its half-detached tail shakily trailing behind.

"Swish! Swish!"

Spurred on from behind by Maternal Grandmother's hoarse voice, it had already slid past the well and crossed the backyard. Before it now was the bamboo grove, densely overgrown.

"Thank you, dear. Just trust your brother to take care of all the household, and think only of keeping your body whole for your long, long journey. Don't worry at all about what you're leaving behind here, but take good care of yourself. That's a good boy. Thank you, dear."

Maternal Grandmother saw the snake off with earnest entreaties, standing beside the well, until it completely disappeared through the bamboo trees and the bamboo shoots which had sprouted thickly during the long rain.

Jinku's father arrived with a doctor from a neighboring village. Paternal Grandmother regained weak consciousness several hours after she had fainted. On waking up from her stupor of a few hours, she looked around the room like one who had been on a few months' trip to a faraway place.

"Is it gone?" were her first words after regaining consciousness. Paternal Aunt quickly understood and nodded. Paternal Grandmother lowered her eyelids, as if to say that was all that mattered. Paternal Aunt quickly recounted all that had happened after Paternal Grandmother had fainted away. She told how Maternal Grandmother chased away the neighbors and reasoned with the snake under the persimmon tree and made it come down from the tree by burning Paternal Grandmother's hair, and saw it off every step of the way until it disappeared through the bamboo grove. Mother occasionally added details to Paternal Aunt's account. Paternal Grandmother was quietly weeping. Tears gushed endlessly from her eyes, flowed down her sunken cheeks and wetted the pillow case. After she had heard all, she told Father to go and ask Maternal Grandmother into the inner room. Maternal Grandmother, who had been resting in the guest room, followed Father into the inner room. It was the first time Maternal Grandmother had stepped into the inner room since the unhappy day of the clash between the two in-laws.

"Thank you," Paternal Grandmother said huskily, raising her sunken and lusterless eyes to Maternal Grandmother.

"You're welcome." Maternal Grandmother's voice was also tearfully husky.

"I heard it all from my daughter. You did for me what I should've done. What a hard and fearsome thing you did for me."

"It's all past now. Don't exert yourself any more

with talking, but try to collect your strength.''

"Thank you. Thank you so very much." Paternal Grandmother held out her hand. Maternal Grandmother took it. The two grandmothers just held hands for a while, and could not speak. Then Paternal Grandmother expressed her remaining worry.

"I wonder if it went on its way all right."

"Don't worry. It must have found a comfortable place by now, and be keeping a protective eye on this house."

Even that brief conversation drained Paternal Grandmother's strength, and she panted. Everyone sat around her till she fell asleep with difficulty and then, leaving only Paternal Aunt to watch over her, we all came out of the inner room to breathe a little.

Paternal Grandmother fainted again that night. She vomited back the few spoonfuls of broth and herb medicine we had spooned into her mouth. From the next day, it was as if her consciousness was playing hide-and-seek in and out of her body like a playful urchin, and there was not a moment's ease for anyone in the house.

Grandmother struggled on for a week, though she had lost control of her body. On the last night of the seventh day, the old lady who always thought more of the son away from the house than the son at home closed her eyes softly, like a spent candle flame quietly subsiding. It may be that in Grandmother's long life the happiest and proudest times were the few days she commanded and scolded the family with amazing vigor, without sleeping and without eating, in rapturous expectation of her younger son's return — like the last radiant soaring of the candle flame before quite sinking down. On her deathbed, Grandmother held my hand and forgave me all my misdeeds. I also in my heart forgave her everything.

It was a long, wearying rainy spell indeed.

Translated by Suh Ji-moon

Fuel

1

Father looked extremely reluctant to set off, as if he'd had a premonition of what was going to happen. And I didn't wonder at it, because, as far as I knew, it was the first unlawful thing Father ever undertook.

Even then I knew. I knew that what Father and I were going to do was close to theft. To put it more bluntly, it was a theft beyond any doubt.

"You shouldn't so much as touch a hair on anything belonging to other people," Father had once said when I reached out to pull up a fat, juicy-looking turnip growing on the edge of somebody's field, to placate my howling stomach, while I was pulling up dried crabgrass vines on the edge of that field for fuel. Father's words put a brake on my appetite and made me feel so ashamed that I could only pretend to be preoccupied with pulling up the tough old dried vines.

Compared with a turnip, what we were going to steal that night was of far greater consequence, grave enough to cause both Father and me to serve a prison term if caught. Father had changed greatly. However, my whole family, from my mother down to my younger siblings, welcomed the change in him. Father was the only one who was grieved about the change in himself. And Father seemed to regard us, his family, as villains conspiring to drag him down from the lofty heights of moral intergrity into the depths of depravity.

"Eat your fill. If you're hungry you're liable to lose courage," Father said, as he spooned up a big portion of his food and put it in my bowl. The meal itself was no heartening fare; it consisted of a mixture of mashed sweet potatoes and a little rice. Mother called the dish "rice mixed with sweet potatoes," but it would have been more accurate to call it "sweet potatoes mixed with rice." In any case, I didn't try to dissuade Father from giving a portion of his meal to me. It was true that if I lost courage, the consequences might be grievous indeed.

We finished the meal in anxious silence. Father made up for the portion he had given me by drinking the liquid made from boiling the burned rice at the bottom of the pot. Then he stepped down to the yard, which was already pitch dark. When I stepped down a moment later, Father was waiting for me, ready to start. Father had his A-frame carrier with a rush mat spread on it slung from his shoulders, and he handed me a straw sack with shoulder straps attached to it.

"Do you feel all right?" Mother asked anxiously.

"Yeah. I was a little bit worried, because it's been such a long time since I used an A-frame, but now I remember how I used to handle it," Father said, with feigned nonchalance. I was glad that there was no moon that night to show us his face.

"Be careful not to get caught!" Mother whispered fretfully. She had shown no anxiety whatsoever when she nagged and scolded Father into undertaking that night's expedition, demanding to know if Father meant just to stand by and watch his family freeze to death.

But that night, Mother's voice was sick with misgiving.

"Don't be stupid!" Father snubbed her harshly. She must have touched his gravest fear, one he didn't want to admit even to himself. Otherwise, Father wouldn't have spoken so gruffly.

We walked out of the gate. Father walked on ahead and I followed. The pitch darkness, which made it impossible for me to see anything, however near, threatened to separate us. There was not a glimmer of a star in the sky.

Even though I had my face and neck well wrapped in mufflers, the wind that swept over field and hills with an eerie whistling struck my cheeks and nose with a keenness that made me clench my teeth. It was unmercifully cold.

"Stay right close to my back," the wind whispered, imitating Father's voice. I obeyed and walked right behind Father with my neck drawn in like a turtle's. But it was not the wind. Father was walking ahead of me, screening me from its dagger points. Father's back looked to me broader than ever, broad enough to fill my whole view.

"It's cold, isn't it?" This time, Father spoke, imitating the voice of the wind. I had been determined to say "no", if Father ever asked that question, but the cold deprived me of my senses for the moment and I answered, like an idiot, "Yes".

"I'm sorry," Father said, in a weak voice. While I was groping for something to say, Father went on, "I meant to save you from death by freezing, but here I am, freezing you to death."

The stone flues of our *ondol* floor didn't warm up. Since it was mid-winter, there was no way we

his pistols and hand grenades that he gathered up. Everybody moved at once.

"I won't let you go, never, now that you're in my house!"

I opened my eyes at last. In that sudden turmoil, nobody paid any attention to me slowly raising my body and sitting up. Uncle's face was covered all over with a bushy beard. Father and Aunt were on either side almost hugging Uncle, who was sitting leaning against the wall on the warmer part of the floor. Grandmother snatched Uncle's arm from Aunt and, shaking it to and fro, entreated, "Because your brother told me lies I thought you were staying comfortably somewhere. I thought you spent your days sitting on a chair in a town office somewhere doing things like giving hell to harsh constables. But now that I know the truth I won't let you go back to such a dreadful place! I'd die first rather than let you go!"

Grandmother wept, stroking Uncle's cheek with her palm.

"I'd let you go if I could go with you and look after you day and night, but since it seems I can't, I'll tie you down in this room and not let you out of my sight day or night. Why can't you stay at home, farm the land, get married and let me hold your children before I die?"

Aunt opened her lips for the first time in my hearing that night and talked to Uncle about the joys of married life, and Mother assented in support of her sister-in-law. Father talked again. He explained minutely what the drift of the war was, and tried to make Uncle realize that he was being deceived by the empty promises of the Communists. He said further that as he knew a couple of people in the police there would be ways to get Uncle released without suffering bodily hurt. But Uncle at long last opened his mouth only to say, "Are you, too, trying to trick me into it?" and shook off Father's hand.

"What do you mean, trick you?"

"I've heard all about it." Uncle said that the police slaughtered all the people who went down the mountain to surrender, decoyed by promises of pardon in printed handbills. Uncle said that promises of unconditional pardon and freedom were screaming lies and tricks.

"And you, too, are trying to push me into the trap?"

"What?" Father's arm shot up in the air. The next moment there was the sound of a sharp slap on Uncle's cheek. Father panted furiously and glared at Uncle, as if he would have liked to tear him apart.

"How dare you strike my poor boy!" Grandmother wept aloud, covering Uncle with her body. Father drew the tobacco box near. His hands shook as he rolled up the green tobacco. Uncle dropped his head.

A cock crowed. At the sound Uncle lifted his head in fright and looked around at the members of the family. The short summer's night was about to end.

"I've killed people," he murmured huskily, like one who had just set down a heavy load he had carried a long, long way. "Many, many people."

Thus began Uncle's wavering toward self-surrender. It was a long persuasion that Father carried out that night, and the patience he showed for it was truly remarkable. At last everything was settled as

Father had planned, and it was agreed that Uncle was to remain in hiding for a couple of days until Father obtained assurance from the police for Uncle's safety. Uncle was to go into the dug-out cave in the bamboo grove that Maternal Uncle had used for hiding under communist occupation.

Everything was settled, and all that remained to be done was for everybody to snatch a wink of sleep before it was broad daylight. But that instant Uncle, who was about to pull off his shirt, suddenly bent forward and pressed his ear to the floor. Grandmother almost jumped from fright.

"What is it?"

"Ssh!"

Uncle put his forefinger on his lips and eyed the door of the room. Everybody's face stiffened, and all listened attentively for noise from outside.

"Someone's there."

My ears caught no sound. There were distant chirps of grass insects, but I could hear nothing like a human sound. But Uncle had his ear still glued to the floor and didn't seem likely to straighten up. I heard for a while only the loud pounding of my heart in that suffocating tension, but I caught a certain sound that Uncle must have spoken of. That sound which distinctly was not the sound of a heart pounding, was footsteps treading ground with long intervals in between. They were so soft and careful that it was hard to tell whether they were approaching or receding.

"Who's that outside?"

Father's voice was low, but the reprimand was severe. Then the sound of movement stopped altogether. Suddenly it occurred to me that it was a familiar tread, of someone I knew very well. I quickly ransacked my brain, trying to work out who it might be. The footsteps began again. They seemed to be moving a little faster this time. Uncle's body shot up erect. Within the blinking of an eye the dark shape jumped over my seated form. The back door fell to the ground with a shattering sound and Uncle's big bulk rushed away in the dark. He had already crossed the bamboo grove. His motion was so swift that nobody had had a second to say a word.

I came out through the frame of the back door that Uncle had knocked to the ground. I ran past the kitchen into the inner yard. I wasn't at all afraid, even though I was alone. I surveyed everything within the twig fence from the yard and the kitchen garden down to the gates, but I could see nothing. When my eyes fell on the unlighted guest room, however, I caught the half-opened door of that room closing noiselessly, shutting out the dim, whitish glare of the morning. I savoured the discovery with rapture. It was indeed a familiar tread, of one I knew very well.

"I'd have packed things for him to take if I'd known it would come to this! I didn't feed him a morsel, nor give him one clean garment! If only I'd known! How could I have not fed him one bowl of warm rice! If only I'd known!" Paternal Grandmother wailed, beating her chest. Paternal Aunt grasped my hand tightly and pulled me to one corner. Then she poured her hot breath into my ear.

"You mustn't tell anyone your uncle's been home. Do you understand? If you talk about such things to anybody all of us must go to jail. Do you hear?"

Village people were surrounding my house, stand-

could remove the floor to clear the flues, so we cleaned the stove and tried to remove the soot from the flues as far as we could reach with a long stick wound with clothes at the tip, and we swept the chimney as well, but the flues refused to carry heat from the stove. On the contrary, the flues threw the flames back into the stove if we lit it. So, all the members of my family caught cold and suffered from watery discharges every night, as from diahorrea. Shortage of food was grave, but the blocked flues were an even greater agony.

Then a neighbor of ours suggested a solution. He said if we burned green pine boughs, which produce fierce flames and heat, it might clear the blocked flues. My mother thought the method well worth a try, and worked to persuade Father to undertake the task of collecting pine boughs from the protected mountains. Father had been staying cooped up in our house, trying to reveal as little of his existence as possible, because the authorities still refused to issue him a certified ID, on account of his younger brother having been an active communist partisan. My mother branded my father a lazy and irresponsible head of the family, who would rather watch his wife and children die of cold than lift a finger. So finally Father and I — the eldest son — departed on an unlawful mission to cut pine boughs from the protected forest.

We arrived at the Soradan Peak, our destination, without incident. It was far from our house and dangerous in the dark, but then it would have been risky for Father to venture even this far out in broad daylight, as he was forbidden by the authorities to engage in social activity of any kind. Moreover, Soradan Peak was a place Father once covered inch by inch in search of the corpse of my uncle, who might have been killed in a raid made by the army of the Republic. Father must have felt bitter about going to such a place to steal pine boughs in the depth of night. The fact that my uncle's corpse was never found couldn't have put Father's mind at ease.

However, we had to go to Soradan Peak, because we were in desperate need of pine boughs, and Soradan was the nearest pine forest.

Setting down his A-frame in a hollow as remote from the forest overseer's office as possible, Father immediately began chopping. Since we had only one sickle, I stood lookout while Father lopped the boughs. I could see nothing, but I could hear everything too clearly. The noise Father made drove me crazy. The sound of the sickle chopped up the sound of the wind. Then it hacked the mountain peak into pieces, and finally hacked at my bosom, shattering what courage I'd had into smithereens. Whenever a pine bough fell screaming to the ground, I felt goose pimples break out all over me. Father was in too much of a hurry. Like one determined to be found out, he was waking up the whole mountain and valley with his hacking. He made as much noise as if he were splitting rocks with a hammer and anvil. The noise drove all sense out of me, and I forgot my duty as lookout.

"You there, don't move!" A voice thundered and a flashlight struck my father. Father seemed to leap up, like a roe deer hit by a bullet.

"Who are you?" The voice came again. The whole valley reverberated: "Who are you?"

"I can't answer, unless you turn off the flashlight," Father said, screening his face with the arm that held the sickle. Perhaps it was because the sudden light was too much for his eyes, but he looked as though he were taking an offensive posture.

"Shut up and show your ID!" the man said, the flashlight still pointed straight at my father. The man also struck the pine trees on his left and right threateningly with his club.

"Who are *you* to demand to see my ID?" Father asked with surprising calm, although you would expect Father to tremble and quail at the mere mention of an ID.

"Oh, you don't know who I am? Well, I'll tell ya. I'm the official overseer of this forest."

"I'm sorry. I left my ID at home."

"Oh, Didya? Well, we'll find out who you are at my office."

"How dare you talk to me in that tone, as if I'm at your beck and call?" This time Father thundered. The mountain reverberated with, "How dare you . . . beck and call?"

"What, has this fellow gone stark mad?"

"Watch out what you say in front of my son!" Father spoke authoritatively again.

The forest overseer broke out laughing. "You wanna be looked up to by your son so much, and you bring him along to this kind of place, to show him how to steal wood from the national forest?" he said when his laughter subsided.

"How dare you use words like 'steal' in front of a young lad? Why don't we let him go home and have a talk, you and me?"

"Certainly not. I'll have to turn him in, too."

"Don't you have children of your own? Would

you like your son to see you humiliated and bullied? Do you think this boy deserves to see his father humiliated?''

"How dare you take that superior tone with me?" The officer raised his voice, but it appeared he wasn't going to insist on turning me in as well. Father made a furtive sign with his eyes in my direction. It meant that I should flee. I ran towards the bottom of the valley as fast as my legs would carry me. After reaching a place where I thought the overseer could not catch up with me, I waited for my father. I hoped Father would make a bolt, too, as I had done.

I waited for a long time, but Father didn't come. Still, I couldn't return home alone. I couldn't go home, unless I could explain to Mother why I came back alone. I started to walk silently towards where Father and the officer were. I thought I would have to look for Father in the overseer's office if he wasn't still where he had been.

Luckily, I met Father halfway up the valley. I could tell, even in the pitch darkness, that Father had his A-frame on his back. I went around to his back without a word.

"It's all right. I'll carry the sack as well."

Father refused to let me carry my share of the load.

"Why didn't you go back home?" Father scolded me. I didn't know what to say. While I was thinking about how to answer, he went on, "You saw, too, didn't you?" I had no time to figure out for myself what he meant, because he went on to say, "You saw how I scolded the impertinent rascal and put him in his place, didn't you?"

I nodded. It was true that I did see him thundering

at the overseer in an authoritative voice. Fearing that he could not see me nodding for the darkness, I said aloud, "Yes."

Father's voice brightened up at once. "I told him he should be able to tell a thief from a gentleman. He apologized for having talked roughly to me. I told him that even though I'm temporarily out of luck, I'm not the kind of person used to going around gathering wood at night, and he insisted that I take home the wood I had chopped down. He even helped me shoulder my A-frame."

Father shook his A-frame, as if to prove it, and the pine boughs rattled, as if in corroboration. I thought to myself it was lucky I hadn't been there to witness Father scolding the overseer and putting him in his place. I wasn't at all sorry I had missed the finale.

"When we get home, you can tell your mother how I scolded that impertinent fellow and put him in his place."

"Yessir."

Father walked on ahead and I followed. There was not a sign of a star in the sky. The pitch darkness threatened to part us.

"You walk right behind me," the wind said, imitating Father's voice. I obeyed. Then, Father's voice said, imitating the wind, "It's awfully cold, isn't it?"

"Yes," I said, before I understood the question properly, and realized again that I had made a grave mistake.

2

The pounding of my heart was killing me on that first
night I sneaked into the railway station yard. In those
days, railway police stood sentinel at the station with
loaded guns. Avoiding the columns of searchlights that
poured coldly over the rails, we crept along the pebbly
bed of the rails and jumped from crosstie to crosstie.
My heart was turning somersaults in my chest, and I
was completely powerless to control it.

"Don't make a noise!" Kil-bong, our leader, stole
to the tail end of the file where I was and whispered
to me, gnashing his teeth. I didn't think I had made
any noise, so I protested, "I didn't!"

"You're gonna get it. If you make one more noise,
I'll kill you!" Kil-bong said, shaking his fist in my face
and gnashing his teeth once again. Creeping along at
the end of a file of cohorts, all of whom grasped iron
hooks and hung cloth sacks from their belts, I thought,
how convenient it would be if one could take out one's
heart and leave it at home when going on a coal-raiding
expedition. That was the first night I had joined my
friends in the enterprise.

"Be quiet, you!" someone cautioned me again. It
was Song-kun, who was crawling along the ground
right in front. He was a year younger than I. Only at
his words did I realize that it was *my* iron hook that
had knocked away a pebble.

After we jumped into the shadow of the freight
cars, my friends grew suddenly agile and bold. Bigger
boys climbed onto the top of the cars, and even the
younger boys pushed their iron hooks into the crevices

between the car doors and the frame. Our leader, Kil-bong, was just marvelous. Lying face down on the open top of the car, he quickly filled his sack to bursting with oval briquets, handed it to one of the group, and filled the sacks of several of his followers as well. I could not but be awed by his feat. As for me, my heart beat so wildly that I dared not even attempt to follow the others and just picked up the briquets that the other boys had spilled on the ground.

On that first night, I didn't get a share. The system was for everybody to carry out as much coal as possible, and on reaching a safe spot, to put all of it in a heap, to be divided by the leader according to each one's age, skill, etc. When at last it came my turn, instead of giving me some coal, Kil-bong gave me a hard box on my ear, so hard that sparks flew out of my eyes. However, my reverence for him did not diminish one iota.

I was not allowed to join the group after that night. Kil-bong flatly refused to have me on the team. There was nothing to do. It was unthinkable for me to go on a coal raid on my own, without the leadership and protection of Kil-bong. While patiently waiting for his wrath to abate, all I could do was to pick up the stray briquets spilled by running trains.

My steadfast loyalty at last bore fruit, and I was given one more chance to prove myself. I vowed again and again that I would gladly consent to have my jaws split if I made the least noise or did anything stupid as I had on the first night. To repay Kil-bong's generosity in allowing me back in the gang, I had to make a desperate effort to earn my share.

As the expedition was repeated, I improved most

remarkably. I became bold and fearless, and this job, which had been no less than torture, became a secret thrill, a pleasure that I would exchange for nothing else in the world. Naturally, my allotted share grew, to the envy of others in the group. Oh, it was only fair and just that each got a share commensurate with his ability and contribution. Now, I was second to no one but Kil-bong in dexterity and boldness. So, when Ching-won, a neighborhood boy and a former class-mate of mine, fawned on Kil-bong in hopes of joining the group, I was the one who most strongly opposed allowing him in, on the grounds that newcomers posed too great a hazard. At last, Ching-won was allowed to join the gang, after repeatedly vowing, at my coaching, that he would gladly have his jaw split in case he caused any trouble or anxiety for the group.

It was a night of a heavy fog. The fog was so thick that we could not see the steam that belched from the whistling, fuming steam-engines as they changed tracks to load or unload. It was an ideal night for coal-raiding. I was put in charge of Ching-won's jaw as we approached the freight cars, creeping silently to avoid being detected by the armed sentries who would fire their carbines into the air if they heard the slightest noise or saw the least suspicious movements. I was authorized to split Ching-won's jaw if he so much as rustled or panted.

But Ching-won was surprisingly composed. Nothing happened until we got quite near the freight cars. If we crossed just one more track, the rest would be routine. But a loud clanging arose right under our feet. It was the noise made by the remote-controlled movable rail, as it slid back to join the main rail. At almost the same time, Ching-won emitted an ear-splitting scream, as loud and prolonged as a train whistle. Our hearts tumbled.

"Shut up!" Kil-bong gnashed his teeth.

"Shut up!" I also whispered threateningly.

But Ching-won didn't stop screaming.

"You idiot!" I swore, and crept towards him, to teach him a lesson. But at that very moment Kil-bong suddenly straightened up and whispered, "We'd better run!"

I also straightened up and began to run, saying to Ching-won, "You'll get it!" The screaming stopped only then. But, even though everyone was running for dear life, Ching-won remained prostrate over the rails and made no movement. Only then it occurred to me that it may not have been just the clanging that had so frightened Ching-won. But by that time, I was already running for my life.

I looked back after we had escaped through a hole in the wire fence of the station. Ching-won was still nowhere to be seen. A train was approaching from the north, led by a hazy headlight. I knew that it was to run on the rail just joined.

The news of Ching-won's death shocked the whole town. Ching-won couldn't escape, because his heel was caught in the switching rail. Villagers rushed to the station belatedly, but Ching-won wasn't there any more where the train from Seoul had passed. Ching-won had already disappeared; he lay scattered everywhere.

That night, my father flogged me with a switch till almost dawn. Between every stroke, Father repeated, time after time, "Who told you to join the gang of thieves? Was it me, was it your mother?''

At last, Father handed the switch over to me and rolled up his trouser legs. I was amazed to see that tears were streaming down his face.

3

From early spring to late fall, our town was all excited with a fever for peat. Peat had been discovered in the rice paddies beyond Grail Mountain.

I still can't understand why my family had to worry about fuel so constantly, when we had so little to cook with it.

Even though it had been quite a few years since the end of the war, my father still loafed at home, unable to find employment. My uncle's support of the Communists during their brief occupation had bound my father hand and foot, and he was little better than a prisoner on parole. My family suffered from shortages of countless necessities.

The rumor that you could shovel up peat from the ground, therefore, was not to be taken lightly. Not only was peat cheap, but it burned slowly, so that it was economical in many respects. Fuel logs were a luxury we couldn't dream of, and we were sick of burning dried grass. One day Father said suddenly, ''Let's all go and dig peat.''

That day, Father brought a long rod from somewhere and sharpened the end of it. He said that if you stuck it into rice paddies, you could tell which spot had more peat and which less.

''You have to use your head in everything,'' Father said triumphantly.

"Oh, is it because you used your head so wisely that you're reduced to digging up earth for fuel in this broiling weather?" Mother snubbed him, as was her habit, but Father didn't talk back. He smiled faintly, as if to say, "You just wait and see."

The vast field unfolding from the foot of Grail Mountain was swarming with people, like a huge stew pot. There were innumerable square holes dug in the rice paddies, and people were shovelling up peat, putting it in baskets, and carrying it home. It was like a busy marketplace.

Trying not to be seen by the owner of the paddies, Father carefully stuck his rod into the bottom of rice paddies. The paddy owners strictly forbade such exploration. The rule was that you had to select a spot simply by the look of the surface. So, there was no telling which spot was more likely to contain high-density peat and which spot was mostly just earth. It all seemed a game of pure luck. So I thought Father's method a highly commendable one. At last, Father selected a spot, which he said contained high-density peat. Father had the owner of the field brought over, and bought four square yards of it. Throwing off our jackets and shirts, Father and I began digging at once.

We drove stakes in the four corners to mark our territory for the day, and began to shovel off the surface earth. Our devoted labor under the broiling sun was rewarded, and soon a layer of yellow peat was revealed. The moment Father shovelled up a cake of peat the size of a football, my mother and my younger sisters and brothers all shouted with glee and clapped their hands. Father was smiling triumphantly, as if to say, "See?"

"You have to use your head in everything," Father said aloud. It was true. Because Father had used his brains well, in the form of a sharpened rod, we were having success. Our little plot had a much thinner layer of surface earth than others. I felt a great pity for those who lacked the sagacity to locate peat-rich spots and had to expend such vain effort shovelling off layer after layer of earth. We were quite some distance from where the crowds were busily digging earth, but we didn't feel lonely at all. We felt only rich and happy.

"Why don't you go bring me some rice wine?" Father asked Mother, wiping the beads of perspiration on his forehead with a towel. Rice wine was so obviously beyond our means that Father hadn't had it since I couldn't remember when.

"Do you think digging up some mud entitles you to royal treatment?" Mother said, casting a petulant glance into the hole. But without any more protest she dashed off to a nearby village. Perhaps Mother was exhilarated and happy too.

Peat is a very strange thing. The top layer was slimy and dripped a thick, dark, stinking fluid. But the deeper you dug, the drier it became. It was yellow-brown. Sometimes, twigs of strange shapes, which must have been buried in the earth for tens of thousands of years, were exposed. If you touched them, they crumbled silently into powder, half-earth and half-peat.

The effort it cost to shovel up the peat was nothing compared to the effort it took to carry it home. Except for Father, all the members of my family were exhausted from the labor of making trip after trip home under the broiling sun with peat-filled sacks. Not only were the sacks heavy as grindstones, but the smelly fluid ran down our backs and the stench stung our nostrils. What labor could be more noxious and disgusting than that?

After two trips, I broke down with a sudden stomach ache. But, by staying behind with Father because my stomach made it impossible for me to walk, I saw something that made me forget my pain. Father was still shovelling excitedly, no doubt with the help of alcohol.

"I still have some strength left, thank God, even at my age," Father said, scooping up a big shovelful. The hole was already so deep that Father stood more than waist-deep in it. Looking at the freshly shovelled peat, I discovered something odd. I got frightened. The color of the peat had changed. It wasn't the high-quality yellow-brown peat any more, but was slimy, dark mud as at first. Father seemed so engrossed in his work that he didn't seem aware of the change. I was just about to point it out to Father when I saw the owner of the paddy approaching slowly.

"Hey, what are you doing?" the owner shouted, looking into the hole.

"What? Do you need to ask?" Father said, straightening up, in the tone of one responding to a joke.

"I can't understand. Are you going to bury one of your ancestors in the middle of my paddy or something? Why did you dig such a big hole for no reason? Aren't you tired?"

"What do you mean, am I going to bury one of my ancestors? And what business is it of yours whether I'm tired or not? Even though you own the land, I bought from you as much earth as I can dig up today. So, you'd better not try to stop me digging as much peat as I can."

"Yeah. I wouldn't interfere with your digging up fuel. But why do you have to dig up pure mud?"

"Pure mud?"

Father's eyes dropped to the bottom of the hole. Breathing hoarsely a few times, Father stooped down. He picked up a handful of earth and began to examine it carefully. Not content, he rubbed the earth between his palms, then lifted it right up to his nostrils to smell it, and at last even tasted it with the tip of his tongue. Father flung down the earth in his hand and flopped down at the bottom of the hole. There was no question that that earth contained no peat, but was pure mud.

"Well, if you've dug up all the peat there is, why don't you quit? I'll have to plant barley here this winter," said the owner of the field, who sauntered away, his hands folded at his back.

Father lay limp at the bottom of the hole. Alcohol burned red in his face. Without a single word, Father looked up at the sky. I couldn't think of anything to say to him. We had netted about a third of what other people averaged from other spots. It was the consequence of Father's brain, and Father's rod, having betrayed and spited him.

"Do you believe so, too?" Father said suddenly, out of the blue. "Do you, too, believe that your father is a stupid, shiftless good-for-nothing?" It was none other than me that Father was asking.

"No! It's only because you're unlucky, and the times are bad," I said hurriedly. It was the tune I had heard many a time from Father's lips.

"Well said, clever boy! Ha, ha!" Father laughed, as if in self-derision. His first-born had at last given him laughter.

"Do come in here, my boy. Why don't you and I lie down together and look at the sky? Viewed through this square frame, the sky looks uncommonly beautiful."

I dared not disobey Father's orders. Father's eyes were accurate. It was a beautiful sky. It was clear blue, and a beautiful white cloud was sailing leisurely across it. Perhaps it was true that the sky was more beautiful because we looked at it through the square frame.

"Let me tell you the truth. It's neither on account of the times nor because of bad luck that I'm a good-for-nothing. It's because I'm a stupid fool," Father whispered. The smell of alcohol overpowered me before his whispered breath wound itself into my ears. Lying on the soggy bottom of the hole he had dug, I just nodded.

"Well, let's get out of this grave. What's lost is lost. But I'll make up for it somehow, by whatever means I can. This winter, if we're out of fuel again, I'll keep all of you warm, even if I have to burn this body of mine."

Father crept out of the hole first, and I followed. As he wriggled to get out of the hole, his rump swerved wide in front of my eyes. Looking at his squirming bottom, I suddenly felt hot in my throat.

Translated by Suh Ji-moon

The Man Who Was Left
as Nine Pairs of Shoes

Right from the start, things hadn't worked out as we'd expected. We'd gone overboard in buying a house in Sŏngnam, and had decided to rent out one of the rooms more or less to compensate for our excess. My wife and I were certain we'd be among the best of all the landlords in the world, and we concluded that a person would surely have a dream come true, becoming a tenant of ours. And so we thought we were justified in demanding that our renters be at least as good as we were. Somehow, though, we felt our expectations had all gone awry, one after another. My own sense of betrayal reached a climax when Yi, a policeman whose rounds included my school, came there in his street clothes to look me up. He started talking about our tenant, Kwŏn, who was listed in the ward register as a resident of our house.

"No need to feel obligated. I'm not asking for a formal report every day. Only when he does something a little out of the ordinary — if he goes away somewhere, if someone suspicious comes to see him, if he goes hungry because he's run out of rice or coal, or if he suddenly has lots of money...."

It was clear to me that Yi's notion of obligation was off the mark. As far as I could tell, at least, it wasn't something we had a choice about. But to hear Yi talk, you would have thought the task was something people valued, to the point of fretting in order to obtain it.

"Are you telling me to be your informant?"

"What an embarrassing thing to say!" said Yi, who, unlike most policemen, was a college graduate. He gave a hearty guffaw, then straightaway became serious. "I didn't come here to harp on the duties of a citizen, Mr O. I'm just asking you to be a good neighbor."

"So all I have to do is squeal to the authorities about Kwŏn's every move, and then I can be a good neighbor?"

"Sure," Yi replied, bursting into another guffaw. "But let's drop this talk about 'informants' and 'squealing' on someone. You'll understand by and by, Mr O. You know, it's not very appropriate the way you express yourself about Kwŏn. Are he and his family getting on your nerves? Or maybe you don't like him?"

"There's nothing about him to dislike at this point...."

"Okay, then, check whether he's out of rice or coal, all right? And see what you can do to help him. I have to stay in the background, or else I'd do it myself. Of course, if he's out of rice or coal we can always blame the people who won't hire him. But then what company would want to hire the subject of an investigation? The bigger problem is Kwŏn himself. He's the kind of person who simply can't put up with a legitimate undercover investigation. The fellow who was responsible for him before me found this out more than once. As soon as Kwŏn senses he's being investigated he gives up on everything — job, everyday routine, even his wife and children — and just lies around in his room. He doesn't eat for days at a time, he tosses down the booze, and sometimes he gets wild like an animal, until he's about to go over the edge. Basically he's a decent, kindhearted man, you know. I think you understand by now what I'm saying. If you can help me to do my duty without Kwŏn knowing about it, you can be a good neighbor — no doubt about it. Frankly, I have a lot of affection for Kwŏn — not as a policeman but as a human being. I'd like to help him as much as I can. I think you'll feel that way too before long, Mr O. Could you please do me this favor and be a good neighbor?''

For me to have a lot of affection for Kwŏn — what an awful thought! I'd much rather pay someone a nice fat reward to be nice to him. From the very beginning, our motive for renting out the spare room next to the gate was not human kindness: it was money.

The sight of Kwŏn and his family moving in was no ordinary spectacle but something splendid to behold. It was a Sunday, and I was just getting around to the rare pleasure of a late breakfast when the doorbell rang. My wife went outside and opened the front gate. I could hear her cry of astonishment from where I was sitting in our family room. I went out to see what was going on, and understood right away what the commotion was all about. I was quite surprised myself. There stood a woman dripping with sweat, her chest heaving. On her head was a huge bundle that looked as heavy as she was. A girl who appeared to be about nine standing a short distance from the gate and a much younger boy a couple of steps away from her briefly caught my eye. Their father was far down the steep hill that led to our house, another bundle at his feet. He was just about to have a smoke, but when he saw me, he shoved the cigarette back in his pocket and heaved the bundle to his shoulders. Overpowered by the load, he was barely able to stagger the rest of the way up the hill. If this was indeed Kwŏn, the man who was to rent one of our rooms, he was carrying out the move on his own, like a sneak attack, without asking our permission, and four days ahead of schedule. As he approached, it appeared he might collapse at any moment, so I snatched the bundle from him. It was much lighter than I'd expected. Its enormous size belied the fact that it was a loosely bundled quilt. His children stared up at me apprehensively. They were holding a bulging plastic bag between them, each with a strap in hand, enduring silently despite the considerable strain evident on their faces. My wife, still looking surprised, was sizing up Kwŏn's wife as if weighing her on a scale. She showed no intention of helping her lower the bundle from her head. I noticed Kwŏn was short. I'm of average height, but I felt like a giant by comparison. Kwŏn remained silent, staring attentively at my sandals, so I felt I had to speak first.

"Is there a truck coming with more?"

"No." He lifted his tired eyes and with his hand drew a long semicircle encompassing his wife's head, the bag the children still held, and the bundle I had just taken from him and placed next to the gate. "That's all." He smiled awkwardly.

Things were sticking out every which way from his wife's bundle — kitchen utensils, I imagined. If Kwŏn wasn't joking, then these few household items — a rice pot, a laundry tub, and some bed-ding — were, finally, all that they were moving. It was pathetic, even for people who wandered from one rented room to the next. While I was standing there amazed, the fellow quickly wiped the toe of one of his shoes against the bottom of the opposite trouser leg. He then wiped the other toe in the same stealthy manner. As he looked down at his shiny shoes cleaned of their dust, his expression brightened like his footwear. His shoes were quite new — a luxury item — and suitably shined. But they didn't match his limp summer shirt with its zigzag pattern, which was old-fashioned and too lightweight for the season. If my guess was right, he'd picked it up at a clearance sale.

"This wasn't part of the agreement," my wife whispered when we were once more by ourselves.

"So what do we do? They had to move today anyway, right? And since we're not using the room, so what if they moved in four days early?"

"That's not what I mean."

"Relax. They made a point of promising us the rest of the deposit in a few days. They're decent people — I hardly think they'd play innocent and end up paying us only half the money."

"I felt that way when they signed the rental agree-ment. But I still think they've got a lot of nerve. They know as well as anybody that two hundred thousand *won* is quite a bit cheaper than the standard deposit. And yet they barge in early without permission and give us only a hundred thousand. The more I think about it, they're just not to be trusted. If they can't keep their word on something basic like this, we can't expect them to honor any other agreements in the future. Since you're the one who told them it was okay, you get the rest of the money from them.''

"Now wait a minute — you're the one who chose these people who won't keep a 'basic' promise.''

"How was I to know they'd turn out this way? What am I supposed to do when people put up a front and try to mislead us? And just you wait. They've got something else in store for us.''

"And what's that?''

"She's pregnant. Maybe she can fool everyone else, but not me. She must be five or six months along. Maybe even seven — who knows? I didn't realize it last time because she was wearing traditional clothing, but today I noticed right away.''

"Pretty sharp, aren't you?''

Already my wife was trying to act every stitch the landlady, just like the daughter-in-law who finally becomes a mother-in-law. She couldn't have forgotten the days when we had to roam around from one cramped room to another, but she certainly gave the appearance that she had. She had gotten in the habit of talking about that period of our lives as if it were ancient history, and the present as if it were too good to be true. "What we had to go through to get this house!'' she would say at the end of practically every sentence, clicking her tongue.

Good point. We had gone through a hell of a lot to get this house, and I had every reason to expect my wife to feel a good deal prouder than I about its acquisition.

Before we moved to this house up behind Sŏngnam City Hall, we had lived near Tandaeri Market in a riverside village of tightly clustered, oppressive, twenty-*p'yŏng** lots. Our landlord there, Kim by name, called himself a doctor of Chinese medicine. He didn't display a sign, but from the looks of his patients, his speciality seemed to be skin diseases. He sold a home-made ointment of dubious efficacy, but seemed to be having a hard time making ends meet. This self-styled doctor spent most of his day taking naps. Then around sunset he started drinking. The liquor launched him on a spree that would usually continue past curfew and stir up the village until dawn.

Kim was quite drunk the day we moved into his house. This was the first time we had met, and as we shook hands he greeted me in a raspy voice. The next thing I knew, he had put his arm around my shoulders and dragged me into his family room. I felt as though I were being kidnapped. Long into the night, he bragged about how he had built this fifteen-*p'yŏng* tile-roofed house in the unbelievably short space of a week. His intimidating voice carried to my wife in the room next to the front gate, where we were to live. At one point, while my wife was doing some chores at the pump in the yard, she had heard Kim shout with glee, "Now that we have a teacher and his wife, there's nothing to worry about!" Finally he had told me, "If anyone in your family is suffering from scabies, pimples, an abscess on the back, cankers, or scrofula, let me take care of it." Then he released me to my uneasy wife.

My first meeting with Kim had thus ended without incident. But I wondered why he felt he had nothing to worry about from then on just because we had rented a room in one of the most jerry-built houses

* One *p'yŏng* is approximately four square meters. [Translators].

I had ever seen — for three thousand *won* a month along with a thirty-thousand-*won* deposit. It took me a while to understand that.

The very next day Kim started announcing throughout the village that his new tenants were none other than a teacher and his wife. (Think of that — a teacher and his wife!) There were comparatively few teachers in all of Sŏngnam, and one of these teachers was renting from him — that was what he said. On payday every month he would visit us to collect the rent and utility bill. Before leaving he would borrow a small amount, promising as he briskly departed to pay it back. But it wasn't just on my payday: whenever we met on the street or in the house, he would stick out his hand and extort a few coins from me. My wife was in the most difficult situation of all. If Kim borrowed money from me, his wife would never fail to come to our room and whine to my wife about it the better part of the day. We would never get the money back, she would warn her. She would also scold me for lending so readily to her husband — the kind of guy, so she said, who would exchange his wife's underwear for liquor.

It didn't take long for my wife to get fed up with being "the teacher's wife," though she'd found the title rather agreeable at first. Simply because she was the wife of a teacher, the neighbor women and their small fry didn't give her a moment's peace. Thanks to Kim's fervent crowing, we were treated as a species apart in the village of twenty-*p'yŏng* lots. The women glued themselves to our kitchen door to learn what kind of supper the teacher ate, and didn't hesitate to peek into our room at any hour to see what kind of make-up the teacher's wife used. An endless swarm of ragamuffins gawked inside to see what snacks the teacher's son preferred. It was the same when my wife did the laundry. When she washed clothes next to the pump, the neighbor women flocked near and marvelled at how the detergent foamed up in the water, as if this basic, mundane chemical reaction were some kind of magic.

One day I returned from school a bit late after teaching some supplementary classes. My wife greeted me with a serious expression.

"I think we're going to have to move out of this area."

"What happened this time?"

"Nothing happened, but I'm afraid of the people around here. They're out to cause trouble — I can see it in their eyes."

"Is it the junk dealer's wife?"

"Yes. She followed me to the market again."

This was the neighbor my wife feared the most. She and her husband lived across the alley in a hovel that was half canvas and half mud blocks. Whenever there was a racket in the alley, I would peek through our window and, sure enough, the woman had gotten into a big fight with somebody. Her opponent was usually a neighbor, but sometimes it was her husband or their little six-year-old son. No matter who it was, she would call the other person "Dog!" or "Swine!" And she was constantly threatening to slice off some part of her opponent with her husband's metal-cutting shears, which were as big as a pair of fodder choppers — though all she really had at her disposal were her teeth and fingernails.

The junk dealer's woman hadn't physically

harmed my wife or my son. She had merely shot them piercing looks from a distance on the street, her daughter dangling from her back. That was enough to discourage my wife, though.

One Sunday afternoon, my wife went out for groceries. She was back sooner than I had expected. Flinging off one of her rubber shoes next to the gate and the other next to the pump, she rushed inside huffing and puffing and made a big fuss of locking the door tight though it was the middle of a peaceful afternoon. Her shopping basket was empty, her face was deathly pale, her chest was heaving.

"The junk dealer's wife followed me the whole way," she panted, her feverish breath flooding my ears.

"And so?" I was taken aback, and couldn't help chuckling.

"Now don't you make fun of me! I'm telling you she chased me from here to the market and back again. I was at the butcher's trying to decide whether to buy pork or beef, and something felt strange, so I looked back, and would you believe it? — that woman was standing there with the girl on her back, staring daggers at me with those sunken eyes of hers. I'd seen her in the alley when I left for the market, but it gives me the creeps to think she shadowed me so far before I realized it."

"Maybe she was thinking about buying some meat too after she saw you with your basket. There's no law that says a junk dealer's family has to eat leftover popcorn."

"Will you listen to me! The way she scowled, I thought she was going to swallow me. My heart started pounding, and I couldn't for the life of me buy meat in front of her. So I left, but she tracked me down at the fish shop. I was too frightened to buy anything there either, so I decided to come straight home. I looked back along the way, thinking I'd lost her, but she was still there. She kept her distance, but dogged me just the same. So, I started running — I couldn't help it. I looked back again, and she was running too. She looked like she was gaining on me, even with the kid on her back. The girl was fussing and crying, but the woman wouldn't give up — she chased me right to the gate.''

I quietly rose, opened the window, stuck my head out, and looked past the gate. The woman had planted herself in the middle of the alley, her daughter hanging low on her back. Her eyes met mine squarely. She easily accepted the gaze of an unfamiliar man and seemed determined to engage in a staredown until I retreated. Bewildered, I jerked my head inside and shut the window.

"What on earth is it with her?" my wife pressed me.

"Maybe she wants to be friendly with you."

"I wonder what she's thinking."

I couldn't help repeating myself: "Well, I'm not sure, but she probably wants to be friends with the teacher's wife."

"'The teacher's woman,' 'the teacher's wife,' 'Madam Teacher's Wife' — wherever I go, that's all I hear. I'm sick and tired of it. Why did I have to end up being a teacher's wife!"

Hell! I was caught between a rock and a hard place. After we'd left our home town, her chronic illness (which was also my illness) had settled down for a while, but now she was about to have a relapse. The one reason my wife wasn't so proud of having married a teacher was that most of the husbands of her Edelweiss Club friends from high school earned much more than a teacher did. My wife could never understand how girls with decidedly inferior grades and looks were able to snap up spouses with the "holy trinity" of qualifications — good family, good schooling, good job. It was as if they had cooked up some plot. And because she couldn't understand it, she couldn't forgive them. Her pride was periodically injured, not because of the discomforts and difficulties resulting from my meager salary, but because the Edelweiss members' eternal friendship with one another, ensured by their biennial meetings, was, in her case, mixed with pity.

It was the same with me. Meeting classmates who had gotten ahead at an early age, or who at least had high hopes for advancement in the near future, or who had already made their fortune, didn't sit well with me. I couldn't help feeling victimized at the thought of working as a teacher for thirty or forty years in the hope of becoming, at best, a vice-principal, principal, or commissioner of a local board of education. No matter how I looked at it, I felt it was my bad luck in this unjust world to have ended up as a teacher.

On the other hand, there were people who thought the world of teachers and treated them as special. So, my situation could have been worse, but this was no consolation. I had never acted like a big shot in front of the people of Tandaeri who considered me a great figure, nor had I responded in any way to their adulation.

I gave my wife no hint of what Yi, the policeman, had told me about this man Kwŏn Ki-yong from Andong. I didn't tell her of Kwŏn's whereabouts during the six years between the births of his two children, Ŭn-gyŏng and Yŏng-gi. Whether I liked or disliked him, I had decided to keep it a secret. Kwŏn's family was already out of favor with my wife, and if she had known that Kwŏn was an ex-convict, she would have fainted on the spot. And if she had known that he had served several years in jail for disturbing the peace and even now was considered dangerous and was being monitored by the police, she wouldn't have lived with them a day longer under the same roof.

As my wife had said, Kwŏn's family had performed none of their various obligations as tenants. And of course they had violated the rental agreement from the beginning. However, I couldn't evict them then and there for such reasons. I decided to watch them for the time being, until they committed a critical mistake.

Before long my wife's hunch about Kwŏn's wife was confirmed. My wife finally obtained a confession from the woman that she was six months pregnant. And before I noticed it, my wife had begun counting our coal briquettes, which we stored under the terrace where we kept the soy crocks. She couldn't sleep at night unless she did this every morning and evening. The biggest headache, though, was the children. Why couldn't they consider their parents' situation? Take our little Tong-jun, for example. Before, when we were moving from one rented room to the next, he had always ended up hitting the landlady's child, which prevented us from speaking out as tenants. However, now it was he who was getting slapped around by Kwŏn's boy and girl. This not only aggravated us but put Kwŏn and his wife in a tight spot.

One Sunday Tong-jun was running about in our yard with a big balloon. Kwŏn's kids were hanging around cajoling him to play with them. When in spite of their best efforts Tong-jun didn't respond, they made him cry by hitting him, or scratching him, or some such thing. That really made my wife's stomach churn. Then they went inside, probably to pester their mother. A few moments later Tong-jun came in panting and starting to badger his mother, asking her out of the blue to buy him, right then, the same kind of balloon Kwŏn's children had. Finally, he led her by the hand out to the yard. My wife came back blushing, and now it was she who grabbed my hand tight and dragged me out to the yard. There I saw Kwŏn's children, happy as could be, with several balloons. I couldn't blame a tenant's children for having fun. The problem was, the balloons had the monstrous appearance of huge cucumbers. I recognized their shape at a glance. Sure enough, they were condoms. I can't tell you how indignant my wife was. She told me that for the sake of our son's upbringing, we couldn't overlook an incident this serious. Fortunately Kwŏn went to work on Sunday, so with a feeling of relief I entrusted this matter of the children's upbringing to my wife. She had kept her eyes peeled for just this opportunity, and she instantly ran to Kwŏn's wife insisting that she and her husband maintain the dignity one might expect of reasonable adults.

It was after some wretched hardships that we had taken out a bank loan and bought our western-style house with its slab roof on an honest-to-goodness hundred-*p'yŏng* lot on the hill behind City Hall. Everyone knew this was the most desirable residential area in Sŏngnam. As the lady of such a house, my wife was not that picky in the conditions she presented to prospective tenants. First, tenants must have no more than two children. Second, they must keep their peace. If they could meet these two conditions, my wife would not, for example, begrudge them the use of our appliances or limit the amount of water they could use for washing their blankets, and she would charge them a reasonable amount for the garbage collection, neighborhood night patrol, and other bills.

Now why must the tenants have no more than two children? Well, my wife had heard this *ad nauseam* as she followed an elderly real-estate agent around in search of a room. His words had struck home, and my wife believed that a respectable landlady should insist on such a condition as a matter of course. And why did tenants have to keep their peace? My wife set forth this stipulation in order to provide a quiet environment for her "learned" husband (as I would call myself), who had showed the world that material success was simply a matter of education and that education should be a lifelong process. She was saddened that we had to rent out a room even after realizing our dream of buying a house. At the same time, she was clearly quite pleased to exercise a landlady's rights over her tenants. Even clearer to her was the difference between the people who lived in a neighborhood of twenty-*p'yŏng* homes and the people who lived in a neighborhood of hundred-*p'yŏng* homes. In essence, this difference was the gap between a twenty-*p'yŏng* mind and a hundred-*p'yŏng* mind. Whenever she had an opportunity to talk about our new location behind City Hall, she would emphasize that we lived in a house we had bought through the bank.

Early one morning I encountered Kwŏn polishing his shoes on the stoop of the room next to the gate. If he had simply been brushing them like anybody else, I might have taken no note of it. But he was absorbed in brushing and polishing half a dozen pairs of shoes — each of a different material, color, and style, all lined up on the stoop.

"Are you having a sale?" I asked, half in greeting and half in jest.

"A sale?"

He immediately stopped what he was doing and looked down at my feet. Or rather he gazed at my shoes. His eyes then crept up my pant legs to the front of my shirt, and when they met mine they had a cool gleam. His face glowed a vivid red, and suddenly a cold smile appeared.

"I gather you don't think very highly of me..."

"I guess I was pretty rude. But I didn't mean anything in particular...it's just that all those shoes...you have so many of them..."

Kwŏn clamped his mouth shut, clearly intending to deal with me no more, so I was left with nothing to say. On his right he had gently deposited the shoe he had finished polishing, and now he picked up another shoe on his left, put it between his knees, and carefully began removing the mud between the rubber sole and the leather upper with an old toothbrush. In this way he deprived me of any opportunity to apologize. Even so, I dawdled there for some time, having completely forgotten that as duty teacher for the week I was supposed to go to school earlier than usual. So this embarrassing situation gave me my first opportunity to observe Kwŏn up close. Although he had been my tenant for several days now, I hadn't really been able to see him face to face, because we were both gone during the day and didn't have much free time. Kwŏn was as well equipped as a shoe-shine boy, and he polished shoes as if he had done it all his life. In place of an apron he had spread an old pair of underwear over his lap to protect his only suit. After brushing every speck of mud and dust from the shoe, he smeared polish on a scrap of cloth wound around his fingers and applied it with a circular motion while spitting on the shoe. An even coat of polish followed by light brushing produced a passable shine, and then he polished the shoe to a final luster with a piece of velvet. The result looked terrific to me, but Kwŏn was not satisfied and repeated the process. He sweated as if this were a labor worthy of Hercules. He panted. He spat. And what he spat was not merely saliva but a sticky secretion flowing from a possessed mind — the product of a wild-eyed will to make something more of this shoe, to transform it from something people wore on their feet to a kind of make-up. Kwŏn's hands moved round and round, smartly and ceaselessly, like spindles. Finally the shoe gleamed like gilded metal, and his gaze moved to my feet and then up to my face. He smiled broadly, his eyes as dazzling as the shiny toe of his shoe. Those eyes, in fact, were his best feature. Kwŏn looked prematurely old. His skin was rough and wrinkled, his beard sparse. He had a protruding forehead and high cheekbones, and his bushy eyebrows almost met. His abnormally broad nose was crooked like a journeyman boxer's, and his lips were as thick as those of Mr Slice (a fellow teacher so nicknamed by the students because a slice of one of his lips would practically have filled a plate). Kwŏn was saved by one feature alone — those large, attractive eyes. Clear and delicate, they showed no trace of viciousness or violence.

Yi the policeman visited me at school again. He said he had merely dropped by on his way somewhere, but it didn't sound that way from his tone of voice. Right off the bat he started scolding me.

"This won't do. It just won't."

"Well, if I had something to report, I would have called you or something."

"Let's call it cooperation rather than reporting. Anyway, you say there's nothing to cooperate with me about so far?"

"Not a thing!"

"Now look, Mr O., Kwŏn quit his job five days ago. How does that grab you?"

"He quit? So he's unemployed again?"

"That's right. He ditched his job with the publishing company. And this time the circumstances are a bit different. Instead of yielding to the authors and doing whatever they requested, he kept trying to correct them and kept pointing out their mistakes. So the president of the company called him on the carpet in front of everyone and warned him: 'Who do you think you are? How dare you challenge these distinguished authors!' He hasn't shown up for work since."

"He looked like he was leaving for work as usual this morning...Yesterday too..."

"Now you know why I asked you to keep an eye on him?"

"But if you can just sit at your desk and see everything with your x-ray vision, why do I have to go out of my way to cooperate with you?"

Yi gave me a knowing smile. "It's significant that Kwŏn is unemployed again. I think from now on you'll begin to see what your responsibility is. The two of us shouldn't rest easy until he finds a job."

I was tired of insisting that I had no reason to oversee and protect Kwŏn. If I had done something wrong, it was only to rent a room to his family, and Yi understood that as well as anybody. After talking about this and that, we returned to the topic of Kwŏn.

"Was Kwŏn one of the people who cooked up that incident back then?"

"I don't know the details; it happened before I joined the force. But it's clear he wasn't so much the brains behind it as one of the instigators. The evidence he left us couldn't have been much clearer. We have photos of people turning police jeeps upside down and burning them, photos of people throwing rocks, photos of people commandeering a bus and speeding down the street in it, and Kwŏn was right in the middle of it all."

"That's hard to believe. Are you telling me that someone who can't even carry a bundled quilt spearheaded a riot!"

"Well, as soon as he's unemployed he skips a meal as often as he eats. You can believe that, can't you?"

"He can support himself. What's the big deal if he skips a meal? Maybe he's not hungry."

"My dear teacher, please don't pretend to be so

coldhearted. Like I told you last time, I'm sure you'll end up loving him too."

As if Yi had no idea what a chore it was to love someone, he laughed confidently and left. He seemed to think that loving your neighbor was as simple as taking coins from your pocket. For some time now a somber voice had been echoing in my mind when I was alone: "Love your neighbor, love the people of Tandaeri, love the people with the twenty-*p'yŏng* lots..."

It was right after the incident I'm about to describe — an incident that truly shocked me — that I decided to leave Tandaeri. I was on my way home from work, and not far from our house I saw a boisterous group of children playing next to the sewer ditch. Our little Tong-jun was among them. I proudly watched him from a distance, marvelling that he was grown up enough to pal around with the neighborhood kids. His face looked unusually pale, perhaps because the other faces were so dark. The junk dealer's boy, in particular, looked as though he had just crawled out of a chimney. Tong-jun shouted something to this soot-faced boy, who responded by dropping to all fours, as if in starting blocks, and then hopping like a frog. Tong-jun threw something in front of him, and then I noticed that this little rascal of mine was holding what looked like a box of cookies to his chest. The junk dealer's boy picked up the cookie from the ground with his mouth and crunched into it without attempting to shake off the dirt. When he had finished it he grinned, displaying his white teeth, and resuming his position in the starting blocks. Tong-jun again shouted something to him. This time Sootface propped himself off the ground on one arm, took hold of his nose with the other hand and started turning in circles. But after a few vigorous revolutions he fell on his face. He got up, spun some more, then collapsed again. It looked as though he would fill Tong-jun's order, no matter how many trials it took. I couldn't keep track of the number of revolutions, but after the boy was finished he was too dizzy to stand up straight. Next, Tong-jun spat on a cookie and threw it on the ground. Then he tried to persuade the other kids to join in. But they merely looked on in a circle with their mouths watering. Perhaps they were dispirited at Tong-jun's demands, which had become more and more severe. Tong-jun now held up a cookie and threw it as hard as he could toward the stream that ran in the ditch. With no hesitation, the junk dealer's boy slid down a cement pillar to the edge of the stream. I had known about this stream for a long time. Factory wastes and sewage from houses collected there and were carried to a larger stream that fed into the Han River.

This was all I observed. Who knows how long the game had been going on? I went to Tong-jun, snatched the box of cookies from him and threw it into the stream, then slapped the little rascal silly. I also wanted to give the junk dealer's son a sound thrashing, but my efforts were directed toward my own little good-for-nothing instead. After I had slapped him several times it occurred to me to look back, and there was the junk dealer's son chasing the box of cookies helter-skelter down the turbid stream.

That night, after shouting at my wife that we should do whatever we could to get out of this awful neighborhood, I couldn't sleep at all. As I tossed and turned, smoking one cigarette after another, I thought about Charles Lamb and Charles Dickens. These two, who had lived in a distant age and in a land that held no special interest for me, took turns keeping me awake.

These two men were known to have had several things in common besides their first name. Both had an unhappy childhood, and sympathy and compassion for slum dwellers seemed to flow from their literary works. But their personalities in real life were as different as night and day, so it was said — as different as their last names. Lamb remained single, looking after his schizophrenic sister, who had killed their mother. His life was consistent with his writing. Dickens was self-educated and had worked in a boot-polish factory as a youth. But in contrast with Lamb, after he had achieved literary fame and a comfortable life, he supposedly used his walking stick to drive away the slum children who begged him for coppers. If Lamb was right, then Dickens must be wrong, and vice versa. I wanted to be on Lamb's side if at all possible. But I had to admit that I wasn't blameless enough to be able to kick Dickens' butt with impunity.

Like my friends, I believed that we shouldn't despise the poor. But it was all right to look down on the rich. It was only right and natural to do so. Calling me a "humanitarian" was by no means the kind of treatment that might damage a friendship with me. My friends and I were frustrated that various social benefits bestowed by the government did not reach the bottom rung of society. Whenever we met people with dead-end lives — on the street, in a coffee shop, or in the newspaper — we tried to compensate for their pitiable circumstances with vicious insults directed toward the mercenary plutocrats who were raking in money any way they could. We considered it our duty and task as educated people not to ignore the difficulties of those who could go no further in life.

But this was nothing more than a theory. I had to confess frankly that I was deluding myself. Generally our outrage was spurred by the newspaper or a broadcast and then put on display during a conversation at a coffee shop or a drinking place, and that was that. My friends and I carried one or two packs of gum for emergency use as a means to drive off the urchins who went around selling gum, and we lumped together all the young people in school uniforms who sold ballpoint pens or newspapers, summarily judging them to be impostors pretending to be working their way through school. While drinking *sŏju* we dreamed of the day we would drink western liquor. We tossed away tips worth dozens of packs of gum. While riding the bus we promised each other we would one day ride in taxis, and while taking a taxi we promised we would one day drive our own cars. Here was the calculation of Dickens, which was totally at odds with the humanitarianism of Lamb. We could do nothing about the tremendous discrepancies between what we heard and what we saw with our own eyes, or between our words and our actions. All that night I slept fitfully, kicking Lamb's butt in my dreams.

The night of Yi's second visit to my school, Kwŏn's son Yŏng-gi wouldn't stop fussing. He hadn't behaved like this before. It sounded like the boy was having trouble getting to sleep, and finally he was scolded for wetting his bed. Then he was left alone until his crying grew quite shrill. When it became loud enough for us to hear it clearly, Kwŏn's threatening voice resounded through the space between the ceiling and the roof. The more Kwŏn shouted, the more little Yŏng-gi's crying, so unlike that of a three-year-old, took on a sharp edge, as if it harbored a will for revenge. Finally, we were all half awake. "Listen to that racket, and his mother couldn't care less about soothing him," my wife muttered in a sleepy voice. True enough, Kwŏn's wife didn't say a word. In fact, since the Kwŏns had moved in, I hadn't heard so much as a peep out of her.

"Dad had better go away. He'd just as soon go far, far away!"

Kwŏn's pathetic outburst must have startled the youngster, for his breathless crying suddenly stopped. Or rather it tailed off like a clothesline being stretched out, and finally it became a series of sobs that Yŏng-gi seemed to swallow and choke on because of his labored breathing.

The next morning I came upon Kwŏn polishing his shoes again. This time he was more absorbed in his work than usual.

"I'm very sorry about what happened last night."

This polite apology, which was quite unexpected, was directed toward my slippered feet. It was strange: you would have thought he was asking for a reaction to his performance the previous night.

The second day of home-visit week at school found me visiting the parents of my students from Starland Village. One the way there, my home room student guide and I came across a school under construction. Workers toting cement bricks on their backs were filing up and down a bouncing wooden foot-bridge to the scaffolding that towered about the structure's concrete skeleton. Some were stripped to the waist, others had rolled up their pant legs or shirt-sleeves; they all looked attractively rugged. But the one fellow who caught my eye reminded me of a soy-sauce bowl among some large earthenware tubs. His trembling legs were barely moving and I was surprised to see that he was dressed just like an office worker despite such rough work. I walked right under the scaffolding to get a closer look at him.

"Mr Kwŏn — isn't that you up there?"

The moment I spoke a brick fell right at me, but I jumped aside and avoided injury. The man hurried down the footbridge to where I stood. Yes, it was he, all right. When I saw his face, white as a sheet and frozen in astonishment, I realized he hadn't been trying to kill me. The man was a sweaty, dusty mess. You wouldn't have believed the stains and wrinkles on the denim jacket he wore over his beige dress shirt. But his shoes were as they always were: the elaborate shine of the chocolate-colored, enameled leather was the lonely sentinel of Kwŏn's essence.

"How did you know I was here?" he asked.

"It was just a coincidence. I'm on my way to do some home visits..."

He glared back and forth at my student and me. I could have put the proof right in his hands but it wouldn't have eased his suspicion, so I hurried off.

Kwŏn returned quite late that night. He came directly into our family room, took a seat, and plunked down a small bottle of *sŏju* as if he meant to plant it in the floor. He was already half loaded.

"I may not look like much, but I'm an Andong Kwŏn!" His voice sounded rather clear considering he was too exhausted and pickled to budge.

"As I'm sure you know, an Andong Kwŏn gets decent treatment wherever he goes. Your family is originally from Haeju, is it not?"

It was Kwŏn's habit to confirm that I had only one suit and that my shoes were always filthy compared with his, and now he seemed intent on weighing himself against me on the basis of our family names. I merely smiled, hoping that this attempt at friendliness would penetrate his tipsiness and sink deep inside his agitated mind.

"Mr Kwŏn, you look pretty drunk. Maybe you ought to get some sleep. We can always talk later."

My wife was standing outside on the wooden verandah. Her face was sulky and her arms were folded. As I glanced at her I tried to show Kwŏn that my suggestion was purely voluntary and that my subsequent effort to help him stand up was full of good intentions. But he staved off my good intentions, letting his involuntarily half-raised bottom flop back down. He then snapped off the cap of the *sŏju* bottle with his teeth.

"So, you don't want to be pals with an ex-con, is that it? Well, I can't let you off the hook that easily. I'm going to have my say, and then I'll leave you alone."

"Ex-con?"

My wife rushed into the room, her eyes gaping as if she had lost her senses. I might have thought she was crying out in unexpected delight at seeing someone, but it soon became clear that she was not in the least delighted.

"Good heavens! Did you say 'ex-con'? Who are you two talking about? Good heavens. Oh, good heavens!..."

"Ma'am, you didn't know that? Mr O. didn't tell you? It's me we're talking about. Is something wrong? Do I have a funny look in my eyes? Judging from those eloquent expressions of yours, you've never seen an ex-con and a nice, respectable man — that's right, a nice, respectable man — sitting side by side before."

My wife jumped back a few steps, as impetuously as she had rushed in. Kwŏn's glare had frozen her into submission, and she appeared ready to do his bidding.

"There's nothing to be scared of. I don't have the energy to harm a fly. Would the two of you please relax and listen to me? I won't take long."

Until then I had been keeping an eye out for a chance to mollify Kwŏn and send him back to his room. But I had to change my mind after hearing this confession. If I listened to him, I told myself, maybe I could fathom the mystery of how he could dare to disturb the public peace yet claim he couldn't harm a fly.

"I believe Freud said this." Kwŏn guzzled some *sŏju* straight from the bottle. "The saint and the villain are two sides of the same coin. The villain expresses his desires in action; the saint replaces his desires with dreams. That's their only difference."

Kwŏn was about to drink out of the bottle again, so I took it from him, gave it to my wife, and had her prepare a simple serving tray.

"I'm not trying to make the saints look bad in order to whitewash my own situation. But it's true, I've taken great consolation from Freud. I feel as if he wrote those words of consolation knowing I'd turn out to be a convict."

The tray arrived. In addition to the liquor there was some pork stew reheated from dinner and a couple of dishes you might see at any of our meals. The first thing Kwŏn and I did was pour each other a shot of *sŏju*.

"Mr O., I was at least as good a citizen as you — until the day I got soaked in the rain like the rat who fell into the water jar. And of course, my wife was probably as gentle and sweet as your wife. Sure, we had our complaints and suffered some injustices, but the best we could do was solve them in our dreams; we never knew how to express them through action."

I asked my wife to buy some more *sŏju*. The more Kwŏn drank, the paler he turned and the more glib he became.

"My whole life has been one big struggle. Probably someone like me shouldn't have been born in the first place. I could have died of typhoid fever, peritonitis, or one of the other diseases I've had, but instead here I am, scraping along with a wife and kids. And then that house we had in the Kwangju Housing Development. Somehow, nothing's gone smoothly."

Several years earlier, a most persuasive rumor had spread, especially among the have-nots, that a "Shangri-La" was to be built in the Kwangju area, on the outskirts of Seoul. Kwŏn had taken this with a grain of salt. He had tended to believe that a "Shangri-La" was nothing special to begin with. But he had been tempted by the prospect of getting a house, and had overvalued the benefit of being within commuting distance of Seoul. He realized now that he had blundered. In the end, he had scared up two hundred thousand *won*, a hefty sum at the time, and through an elderly, part-time realtor had bought a lot from a displaced family.

"For the first time in my life I owned a twenty-*p'yŏng* lot. I was so happy I paced the boundaries of that lot every morning and every night. I even got down on my hands and knees and measured it — I practically caressed it. I knew the land should have belonged to a displaced family — people more unfortunate than me — but that didn't bother me. At that time, the world didn't look any bigger than twenty-*p'yŏng* to me."

Kwŏn had barely managed to get this land, and now he lacked the wherewithal to lay the foundation and build the frame of a house in order to get some shelter. So he let the lot sit, and for the next several months the family got by with an old tent he had rounded up. It was an election year, and the candidates for the National Assembly added various pledges one after another, to the plans announced for the construction of the "Shangri-La." Magnificent ground breaking ceremonies were held here and there, and a construction boom followed. In no time the paradise for displaced families, most of them day laborers, was at hand. As the election campaigns heated up, land prices skyrocketed, wages jumped, and real estate speculators buzzed everywhere. None of these developments concerned him in the slightest, Kwŏn had thought. But then the elections were over, and in the light of the twenty-watt bulb in his tent, he found out how wrong he had been. The realization was like a jolt of lightning.

"The very next day — can you believe it? The elections were held one day, and the next day it all started."

A notice was delivered from the authorities in Seoul: any lot purchased from a displaced family must have a house on it by June 10, or the sale would be cancelled. June 10 was fifteen days away. Kwŏn and his wife had to build a house on their lot within that period. Since Kwŏn was not a day laborer and his livelihood was still in Seoul, he had gone his own way in Kwangju, indifferent to the chaotic events concerning the housing development that had surfaced during the campaigns. So now he was off to a late start on the house. He had to run his ass off to catch up. First, he took several days off without notifying the publishing company where he worked and tried frantically to scrape up some money. As the money materialized he bought cement, cinder blocks, and lumber. With his wife he started building, one row of blocks atop the next. The two of them didn't know the first thing about construction, but they carried out the enormous enterprise undaunted, their instincts telling them that at least the house wouldn't collapse. More than anything else, they felt lucky and grateful that the authorities didn't ask them to build an attractive house worthy of the name "Shangri-La." When they were out of building materials they stopped working and begged friends and relatives for money to buy more. They repeated this process several times, and before they knew it the walls were up and the roof was on. The whole thing took less than the fifteen days. Whatever its quality or outward appearance, the house the Seoul authorities had decreed was finally constructed.

"We felt like we should have thanked the authorities for making us build the house so fast. For almost a month we were on top of the world — we had ourselves a palace. My wife hugged our little Ŭn-gyŏng, and the tears trickled down her cheeks."

But just as they were about to breathe easy, there was another notice from Seoul. Those people who had bought lots from displaced families would have their ownership officially recognized only if they deposited eight to sixteen thousand *won* per *p'yŏng* for their twenty-*p'yŏng* lots by the end of July. Otherwise, the sale would be cancelled and they would be subject to up to six months in jail and a fine of up to three hundred thousand *won*.

"They gave us fifteen days this time too. There's something they love about fifteen days."

To make things worse, the Kyŏnggi provincial office sent them a notice to pay a real estate acquisition tax. In this manner, the city of Seoul and Kyŏnggi Province, which supposedly had different jurisdictions, would sometimes whistle a different tune on the same matter and in this case both the displaced families and those who had purchased lots from them were at their wits' end as a result. A citizens' organization called the Committee for Correcting the Resale Price of Kwangju Housing Development Land was formed (the name set a record for length in those days), and was straightaway renamed the "Committee for Opposing and Correcting..." Since Kwŏn was known to be a learned fellow, those who were in the same boat as he drafted him onto the original committee and then its successor.

"I suppose you could call this a position of honor, but to me it was more than I deserved."

Kwŏn was not saying this out of humility. Not only did he feel incapable of performing his duties, but because he regarded himself as a Seoulite through and through rather than identifying with the Kwangju Housing Development, he was reluctant to take on the responsibility. And so he didn't attend any of the nonstop committee meetings. Without a hint of a settlement in sight, the end-of-July deadline for payment of the deposit passed in an atmosphere of taut anxiety. And then on August 10 — the day of action decided upon by the committee — things started to happen.

As fate would have it, this high-pressure political atmosphere was greeted with a low-pressure weather system and it began to rain. From early in the morning, leaflets were scattered on the streets and posters appeared on the walls. Yellow ribbons were distributed, to be pinned to the demonstrators' chests at eleven o'clock. Kwŏn remained in his house, not budging, but the sounds of the people moving about outside put his nerves on edge. He sensed that something would surely happen, and that scared him. To Kwŏn, the present situation was better than whatever might happen. The rain fell intermittently. The committee representatives duly presented themselves at eleven o'clock for talks with the authorities, but when the government spokesman did not appear, they decided to wait no longer. Shouts for the citizens to come out into the streets echoed through the alleys of the housing development. "Grab whatever you can — don't come out empty-handed!"

Someone knocked so hard on the sliding door to Kwŏn's house that it almost jumped from its track.

"Mr Kwŏn! Are you there, Mr Kwŏn?"

Kwŏn's heart sank. He had his wife reply that he had left for work. Only after getting rid of this fellow, whoever he was, did Kwŏn remember it was Tuesday. He asked himself why he had been moping around the house since the day before. The answer suddenly dawned on him: it was his dependence on others. His was the attitude of an opportunist — one who never jumped into the thick of things, even when they deeply concerned him, but waited for the moment when the efforts of others bore fruit. Kwŏn was shocked. This was an unequivocal awakening and he was overcome with shame. He sprang up and rushed outside. The streets were choked with people running toward the government branch office shouting slogans and carrying any kind of stick or tool they could use as a weapon. Upon confronting them he ducked into a side street like a thief. He might have joined them, given his awakening, but his eyes kept searching for a bus to Seoul. But it was useless: transportation to the outside had been cut off. During this brief search for a bus, he was drenched to the bone by the relentless sheets of wind and water that beat down on the demonstrators. He gave up on the buses and began searching for a quiet alley. He moved aimlessly, thinking these unfamiliar streets he was walking for the first time would eventually lead him to Seoul. And then he came upon a vehicle with the same goal — a taxi that had avoided the club- and rock-wielding mob by zigzagging through alleys. In desperation Kwŏn jumped into the middle of the alley and blocked the taxi's path. He couldn't have cared less about the fare. He got inside, joining a party of three well-dressed men. The taxi had to pass through the gateway to the housing development, and there it was stopped at a checkpoint. A menacing group of youths armed with two-by-fours, bicycle chains, and other primitive weapons ordered the taxi's occupants out.

One of the youths approached the window where Kwŏn was seated. He bowed, grinned, and spoke congenially.

"Well, well, well, if it isn't our esteemed committee member. Don't you think it's a bit much for you to take on Seoul all by yourself? Would you mind getting out?"

Kwŏn had no idea who this youth was. When he didn't immediately respond, a second youth smashed the windshield of the taxi with a club. The passengers jumped out, and the youths, already hoarse from shouting, raised their voices as loud as they could while threatening the men with their weapons.

"Selfish sons-of-bitches!"

"We've been on a hunger strike and going all out, and look at you sitting in a taxi like you never had it so good!"

"If we go on a hunger strike, we do it together! We eat, we do it together! We die, we do it together! We live, we do it together! Got it?"

By this time the passengers were frightened half to death.

"Mr Kwŏn, how about following me over there?" whispered the youth who seemed to know him.

It wasn't the sight of the clubs but rather the kindness of this youth that scared Kwŏn the most. Fettered by the young man's smile, Kwŏn did not resist as he was led to a weed patch beside the road. There the youth delivered a long lecture. "Of course, as you know..." Beginning every sentence with this assumption, he drew a lavish comparison between the leisure class in Seoul — who at that very moment were eating, drinking, dancing, and tumbling about in bed — and those living in misery in the housing development. Kwŏn realized that this spiel was designed to raise his slumbering social consciousness, just as one of the old songs exhorted the children of the "New Korea" to rise and shine. But not a word registered. Instead, Kwŏn asked himself how on earth a person could be cruel enough to treat him so kindly in a situation such as this. The youth decided that his lecture must have sunk in, and led Kwŏn along a steep hillside that provided a short cut to the center of the housing development.

"It was right over in that area." Kwŏn pointed in the direction of the window.

Regrettably, from where we sat in our family room it was difficult to figure out where he was pointing. Kwŏn realized from our expressionless faces that he wasn't getting through to us, and before I knew it he had sprung to his feet and was out the door. I followed, wanting simply to detain him. At some point Kwŏn's family had gathered at the edge of the verandah near the front door, and they stared up at the two of us as we popped out of the family room one after the other. At the sight of their daddy the little ones burst into tears. Kwŏn's wife, her stomach huge, appeared ready to collapse on the verandah. She gazed in bewilderment at her husband, who had turned as red as a beet.

"You don't have to cry. Daddy's still alive."

I sensed from Kwŏn's low voice that he was well aware of the dignity he enjoyed as a family head. He threaded his way between the crying children until he had reached the yard. He spoke clearly, but staggered as he walked, as if his determination to keep his balance could reach no further than his tongue.

"It was over there," he explained repeatedly. He was much more sure of himself now. A cluster of lights far down the hill flickered beyond the tip of his index finger. They seemed to have poured down from the sky. Although the children must have realized by now that the adults were not quarreling, their torrent of tears did not ebb.

" 'Look at that!' this young fellow shouts. Well, I was already looking. I could see through the rain that the demonstrators had faced off against the police. It was rocks against tear gas. The young fellow was in high spirits — it was almost as if he'd waved a magic wand and created the whole scene. But frankly I wasn't all that impressed by the sight of two groups getting soaked in the rain while they fought each other. I was more worried about what my young friend was going to do to me now that he'd brought me this far. But then everything changed right before our eyes. A three-wheeler loaded with a bunch of ripe yellow melons came along and got swept up in the crowd. It must have taken a wrong turn. The driver nosed it in every direction trying to break out, but it ended up getting turned over on its top. All those melons spilled out and started rolling down the street. Right then and there the demonstrators stopped their rock throwing and swarmed over the melons like bees. The entire load was gone in no time. People were actually picking them out of the mud and chomping in. Eating isn't exactly a pretty sight to begin with, but there was something downright primitive about these people fighting over the melons, and it scared the devil out of me. 'My god, this is human nature at its most naked,' I told myself. I'd never been so moved. I'd always tried to convince myself that I was a different sort from others, but now I wasn't so sure about my reasoning. In fact, I couldn't think about myself in a level-headed manner anymore.''

I had a hunch Kwŏn wasn't going to continue, so for the first time I spoke up.

''Do you mind if I ask what happened next?''

''Why do you need my permission? You've already asked. Three days later a detective showed up at the publishing company and put me in handcuffs. When I saw the photos the police handed me as evidence, I couldn't believe it. There I was sitting on top of a bus; there I was holding a can of kerosene; there I was waving a two-by-four around. It was my face all right, but I'll be damned if I can remember any of that stuff.''

I felt I'd heard all there was to hear. Now I could understand why Kwŏn had invited himself in, clutching a bottle of *sŏju* , and unraveled this tale he had kept to himself. But there was one small matter that still bothered me, and I thought it would be better for both of us if we could resolve it while we had the chance.

''I guess you've known for a while that I've been seeing Yi, the policeman?''

Kwŏn smiled. ''More precisely, he's been seeing you, I would think. You know, when one part of the body is paralyzed, another part becomes uncommonly sensitive. In my case, it's a sixth sense.''

''I hope you don't think I've been informing on you. Yi calls it cooperation, but...''

Kwŏn smiled again. ''There are times when you can do something you wanted absolutely no part of, and not even realize it — remember? Probably you're no exception. Just because you haven't cooperated with him in the past doesn't mean you won't cooperate with him in the future."

"I sure had that Kwŏn figured wrong," my wife whispered to me after we had gone to bed that night. "I thought he was an idiot, but he's something else entirely."

"He wrapped you around his little finger — you were helpless," I replied.

"I know it, and it makes me so mad!"

After I turned off the light, she spoke again in a low voice.

"Her stomach looked bigger than ever today — you saw it. What's the poor thing going to do if it's twins? I know she's only eight months along, but she looks like she's ready right now — goodness..."

"Relax — she's not going to ask you to have the baby for her."

That night I dreamed I was taking turns kicking Dickens' butt and Lamb's butt. And then I was kicking Kwŏn's butt and he was kicking mine.

My wife suddenly began showing an interest in Kwŏn and his family. More specifically, it was an interest in his wife's abdomen, which looked as though it would spill forth at any moment. From the way my wife talked, I gathered the two of them had contact during the day when Kwŏn and I were out. Kwŏn's wife didn't even know her own due date, my wife giggled. When she had kidded her about this, the other woman had casually replied that it didn't matter. When the time came, she would go into labor and give birth — the result would be the same.

Kwŏn hadn't found a job yet. But even without regular employment, come morning he would put on his work clothes and leave the house. I figured that since he didn't have a trade, he was still doing casual labor at construction sites, though he hardly had the strength for it. His two children still made their way into our family room after a lengthy chorus of "Come on, Tong-jun, let's play!" But now they often stood their ground there instead of returning to their mother, even at mealtimes. Here was a sign that the situation in the room beside the gate had become serious. Even so, neither Kwŏn nor his wife had ever opened up to us and asked for assistance. If we hadn't made up our minds to help them after witnessing the shape they were in, who knows how far they would have been driven in their wretched circumstances? Just as Yi the policeman had predicted, I began stealing into their kitchen like Santa Claus and leaving them coal, rice, and such. Whenever I did this, my wife would feel too outraged and victimized to finish her supper. When she thought about the expectant mother and her helpless little children, she insisted that this was the least we could do. But when she realized some of this goodwill of hers might extend to an idiotic fellow who couldn't even provide a decent living for his wife and children, she let herself get so worked up that she had a hard time sleeping. She had already forgotten having whispered to me only a couple of nights before that Kwŏn was "something else entirely," and now she complained to herself over and over about renting the room to him.

Kwŏn's income remained meager, and in no time his wife had reached term. One day I returned from school and my wife whispered to me that Kwŏn's wife had gone into labor sometime after lunch. Then at supper we heard an unfamiliar sound from the room beside the gate. First Kwŏn's wife groaned like someone with the flu, and then, as if a dagger had penetrated deep inside her, she produced a sudden, heartrending cry that soon trailed off. She did this several times. It was the first time I had heard her voice.

My wife thought it was time to get Kwŏn's wife to the hospital. "Can you talk some sense into him, Dear? I tried several times, and he's just impossible! All he did was laugh and tell me not to worry."

"It's not Kwŏn that's refusing — it's their lack of money," I responded.

For some time now my wife had been half critical and half worried about their failure to prepare for the delivery. "A woman with a stomach as big as a mountain having a baby at home in this day and age, and doing it all by herself — the more I think about it, I know something bad's going to happen. A fellow who doesn't even have the money for a midwife, and a woman who's nine months pregnant and hasn't bought a single diaper — what a pair!"

I hurried through the rest of my supper and called Kwŏn out to the yard. Just as my wife had said, Kwŏn immediately began chuckling and telling me not to worry. You might have thought from his tone that he was the one who was trying to comfort someone in a fix.

"She had the second one by herself, and did a beautiful job."

"It's not your family we're worrying about, but ourselves. I'm not saying something'll go wrong, but if it does, I'll hold it against you."

Leaving him with these harsh words, I disappeared inside. What a calculating guy, I told myself. I had discreetly offered to lend him the piddling cost of a delivery at the local clinic, but he had turned me down. I had to conclude that he chose to risk two lives rather than going to the trouble, such as it was, of repaying a trivial debt.

But when midnight passed with Kwŏn's wife in the same condition, the situation changed. Women who weren't first-time mothers didn't have labors that long and relentless. This must have scared Kwŏn, because he left carrying his wife on his back and scurried down the steep slope from our house before the end of curfew. It took a load off our minds to see Kwŏn and his wife stealing out of the room beside the gate. The two of them looked like a drum riding on a pair of drumsticks. Before leaving for school the next morning I asked my wife to buy some seaweed for soup for the new mother, and then to go to the hospital when word of the delivery arrived.

That afternoon Kwŏn came looking for me at school. A class had just started, but I happened to be free that period and was chatting in the teachers' room, so I was able to meet Kwŏn at the front gate as soon as the custodian called me.

"I'm sorry about this — I know you're busy."

Kwŏn tried to keep a smile on his face, but I had never seen him so self-conscious. I interpreted this in a good light: he had just become a father for the third time. I tried to dismiss the ominous feeling that had come over me the moment the custodian notified me.

"Did everything turn out all right?"

"You know, it's a good thing I listened to you. It would've been a disaster if I'd kept her at home. I don't know whether it's a boy or a girl, but it seems like the kid's giving me a hard time in order to teach me a lesson."

He was still smiling self-consciously. His toe was busy in the dirt drawing some word or picture I couldn't decipher. His shoes were astonishingly shiny, considering he had just trudged up a dusty hill to get to the school No doubt he had been wiping his shoes against his pant legs while he was waiting for me.

"Could you lend me a hundred thousand *won* or so?" he blurted right in my face.

His self-consciousness abruptly vanished and a provocative expression filled his upturned face. He had tried to sound as nonchalant as if he were bumming a cigarette. But then while I was trying to recover my powers of speech, his tone became furious.

"They say she has to have a Caesarean. They x-rayed her, and at first they didn't find any complications. Her cervix is wide open. Her water didn't break early, and the fetus was in the right position. And it's not twins. So everything's like it's supposed to be, except that she's been in labor more than twenty-four hours. The doctor said that in a case like that there's only one possibility: the baby hasn't dropped because it's turned inside the uterus and got the cord wrapped around its neck. And shit — that's exactly what happened! If the doctor doesn't do something soon, they're both in trouble."

The only thing that made me ill at ease was the exclamation "Shit!" This word was so uncharacteristic of Kwŏn, but otherwise his explanation was sincere.

Or perhaps it sounded much more sincere because of this vulgarity, which I had never heard him use before.

I couldn't give him a ready answer. His request for "a hundred thousand *won* or so" was too serious to allow me to convey my sentiments through such tactless, banal expressions as "Oh, that's too bad" or "I really don't know what to say." On the other hand, I still had to pay off more than half of the loan I had taken out from my school to help pay for our house. He wasn't talking about ten or twenty thousand *won* — the cost of a normal delivery — and to lend him the huge sum of a hundred thousand or so was simply more than I could handle. And I couldn't go ahead with such a big undertaking without my wife's knowledge, because she was the one who controlled the family purse strings.

"If you can lend me the money, I'll do whatever I have to do to pay you back — whatever I have to do," Kwŏn said. He looked as solemn as if he were swearing on a Bible.

It was a good thing he reminded me. Otherwise it might never have occurred to me that getting the money back from him would be more difficult than finding the money to lend him. How was he going to pay me back doing casual labor or some occasional, low-paying translation work for a publisher, when he couldn't even feed his family? So for me the best thing was to avoid lending him the money out of sympathy. And therefore I had to speak harshly to prevent him from raising objections.

"Which hospital is it?"

"The Wŏn Gynecological Clinic."

"It'd be difficult for me to come up with the cash

right this minute. Why don't you try the doctor at the clinic again? I'll give him a call right away and tell him I'll act as guarantor. Doctors are decent people — they wouldn't let someone die, would they? If that's your only way out, give it a try.''

Because my response was too slow in coming, Kwŏn seemed to have been expecting this. His aggressive countenance softened, and the self-consciousness returned to those fine eyes of his. He shook his head.

"It's too late to pin our hopes on the doctor accepting a verbal promise. From the moment we walked in the door he knew it would't be easy to collect payment from me.''

Kwŏn was sweating nervously, but instead of wiping his face he lifted his right foot and wiped the shoe a couple of times against the bottom of his left pant leg. Then he switched legs and repeated the movement.

"It really is rude of me to bother you when you're busy,'' he said with difficulty. His "Mr Slice'' lips twitched like those of a baby waking from a shallow sleep.

I thought he would say more, but he quickly turned and began to walk away, his arms swinging. Perhaps I was anticipating the moment he would say in a choking voice from deep inside, "Thank you, Mr O. Now you go home and have a good meal and live well the rest of your life,'' or some such thing. I expected the words to fly out of his mouth and stun me. And so I flinched when he abruptly turned back and looked straight up at me.

But this was all he said: "I may not look like much, Mr O., but I'm a college graduate!'' He spoke self-consciously, as a student's parent might do while thrusting a small gratuity in my pocket.

You wouldn't have thought that the arms on that short frame could swing as they did. With every step down the hill he seemed to be cursing the earth and the sky. At the moment he disappeared around a bend in the bare loess of the hill, I was seized with an urge to run after him and call him back. This too is human nature at its most naked, I felt. It was just like when Kwŏn had seen the people in the housing development suddenly stop their rock throwing and run to the over-turned three-wheeler to devour the melons. And then it occurred to me that I was indebted to Kwŏn to a certain extent — that is, if I were to consider his rental deposit as a kind of debt. I don't know why I hadn't thought of that earlier.

At the clinic everything was ready for the opera-tion; all that was missing was the deposit. I had weasled an advance on my salary from the school and emptied the pockets of my closest friends among the teachers, and barely managed to come up with the one hundred thousand *won*. As soon as I handed it to the doctor, he ordered the nurse to bring in the anesthesiologist. When the doctor learned I wasn't a close relative of Kwŏn but only his landlord, he clicked his tongue.

"You get all types of people for fathers. I sent him out for the deposit this morning, and haven't seen him since. Can you believe it?"

"Sure, just like there are all types of ways to deliver babies, there are all types of people fathering children."

I prayed that the doctor in his gold-rimmed spec-tacles would get the point, but unfortunately he chose to take it as a joke, and broke into a laugh. So much for my attempt to be serious.

I helped wheel Kwŏn's wife into the operating room. If she wasn't already dead, she certainly looked it.

For an operation that extracted one life and saved the other life that had kept the first one going, it was over all too quickly. I sat in the waiting room and chain-smoked half a dozen cigarettes, as I had the day our little Tong-jun was born. Finally I heard the baby crying.

"It's a pepper, a little pepper!" the nurse cried out.

The doctor's wife had assisted with the operation, and as she emerged from the operating room she asked me in a loud voice if I'd guessed from the first cry that it was a boy. Then she congratulated me as if I were the father. I had no choice but to play along and praise her for her efforts. A moment later I looked into the face of Kwŏn Ki-yong's new boy, all swaddled. His plump, handsome face betrayed his ignorance of the Caesarean section his mother had just undergone. His voice was loud and resonant, quite in keeping with my initial impression of the man for whom this medical procedure had been named. As I listened to this rugged little fellow cry as though he would lift the whole building, I settled comfortably into the deep emotions of the day our own boy was born.

It was the most peculiar coincidence that we had a burglar that very night. I'd never before had such an experience. As I slept, I felt someone shaking my shoulder. I tried to brush the annoying hand away, but the silent movement continued. Realizing with a start that it was an unfamiliar hand trying to wake me, I opened my eyes, and there in the red glow of the nightlight was a masked man — and the gleaming blade of a kitchen knife pointed right at my neck. The man reeked of liquor. The nightlight tinged the dark shade of the mask with red, and from the eyes and the bit of the nose exposed above the cloth mask I could detect the man's considerable drunkenness.

"Get up. Quick, I said get up."

The burglar spoke in low, measured tones, not wanting to wake anyone else. I wanted to get up, but how? The kitchen knife pointed at my throat was dancing up and down. If the burglar happened to stick me in the neck, the wound would be the accidental result of his excessive trembling. This was a burglar without much experience. The moment I saw his eyes, I realized he wasn't a specialist in this area. Despite all his dutch courage, those large, attractive eyes couldn't hide his inherent decency — or his fear of me. If he hadn't become potvaliant and climbed the wall of our house, he would have flunked his course in felonies from the start.

"I'll be happy to get up if you'll just pull that knife back a little bit."

The burglar did as I asked.

"Give me what you've got. Quick," he whispered while waiting for me to sit up.

"Anything you say. But it'll be easier if you do as I say too."

The burglar shot me a doubtful look.

"There's not much money in the house," I added.

"There's a piggy bank on the bureau, and my wife might have some spending money left — it'd be in the drawer at the bottom of the cabinet. If you can find anything else, help yourself.''

The burglar looked even more dubious, and didn't seem to want to act rashly, so I decided to test him by pretending to be irritated.

''Would you prefer to see my wife get up and scream bloody murder? For your own good you'd better trust me and do as I say.''

The man drew a deep breath and finally started around our bedding toward the bureau. I noticed that this burglar was polite enough to have removed his shoes. He tottered, and wouldn't you know it, he must have stepped on Tong-jun. The boy whined, and the burglar flinched, then hunched over and patted him on the shoulder. The man waited until the little fellow was asleep again. Then he rose, glanced at me to make sure I had stayed put, and got down to the job at hand. I noticed his face was sticky with sweat. Suppressing an urge to burst into laughter as I observed the charming movements of the burglar, I slowly sat up and retrieved the knife he had dropped on our bedding while putting Tong-jun back to sleep.

''I think I've got an idea of how long you've been in this business,'' I said, offering him his weapon.

I thought he would faint from the shock. I gave him a friendly smile and gestured for him to take it. After hesitating a moment, he lunged toward me, snatched the knife, and once more pointed it at my throat. Having detected that our man was not the sort to stab someone on purpose, I had no regrets about returning the knife. Sure enough, he merely stuck it in his belt. His pride had been deeply wounded.

''All this talk of yours, and there's nothing worth stealing here.''

"That's why our friendly neighborhood thieves have given up on us."

"You think I wanted to do this? I was driven to it by circumstances — I couldn't help it."

I decided that this was a splendid opportunity to set his mind at ease.

"That's usually the way it is. Someone in your family has a serious illness, or you get in over your head in debt..."

The burglar's eyes immediately filled with suspicion. He retreated to the verandah, trembling in outrage to the point that his teeth clattered. The smell of liquor that he left in his wake was enough to make me sick. It was clear to me that all he embraced in his hurried departure were the shreds of his pride. So, far from calming him, my approach had only frustrated him all the more.

"There's no law that says you have to go it alone when you've got troubles," I called out to his back. "Who knows, maybe you have a good neighbor who's already made things easier for you."

"Don't give me that crap! I don't have any neighbors like that — I found that out myself! I don't believe anybody now!"

He put on the shoes he had left at the front door. I got up to follow him, fighting the impulse to turn on the light in order to see the shoes. He opened the front door and stepped down into the yard. Then he apparently forgot he was supposed to be an armed burglar who had broken into our house, because he turned toward the room beside the front gate. To spare him more embarrassment in the future, I had to point out his mistake.

"The front gate's over there."

He stopped for a moment before the kitchen, then slowly began walking toward the gate. He began staggering. When he reached the gate he looked back at me. "I may not look like much, but I'm a college graduate!"

Who said you weren't, I asked myself. After this unexpected revelation about his college background, the man opened the gate and was swallowed up in pitch darkness.

I closed the gate but didn't lock it. On my way back in, I peeked in the room beside the gate and confirmed that Kwŏn hadn't returned, and that his boy and girl were curled up in the darkness without their mommy and daddy. My wife was standing outside the front door in her nightgown, her arms folded.

"What's going on?"

"Nothing."

Nothing was missing. Everything was in place on the bureau, including the piggy bank. As I had said, nothing had happened. Before I went back to sleep I told my wife I had paid for the operation. She was silent for a time, then turned toward the wall.

"Don't worry about them running out on us — we've got their deposit."

"Are you sure something didn't happen?"

She turned back toward me. To the end I never mentioned to her that a poor excuse for a burglar had entered our house.

Kwŏn hadn't returned by the next morning. I dropped by the clinic on my way to school. He hadn't been seen there since his departure in search of the deposit for the operation. Nor did he return home the next day or the day after that. It was clear by now that he had left for parts unknown. And I clearly saw that my approach had been boneheaded, despite my good intentions. Upon seeing those eyes above the mask, I had known immediately that the burglar was none other than Kwŏn. At the time, I had decided that I should treat this masked man as a burglar to the very end if Kwŏn were to save face and be his old self come morning when he was sober. And so I expected him to have been able to visit the clinic as if nothing had happened, to see his wife and third child. I regretted not having caught sight of his shoes at our front door. For some reason I got to thinking that I might have foreseen his fate simply on the basis of how well those shoes had been shined. As long as the toes of his shoes had been polished as bright as a glass bead, his pride would have glowed even more brightly and I could have breathed easy.

My coldhearted reminder as he was about to enter the room beside the gate weighed on my mind. What if he had been thinking that this would be the last time he would see his children? And what then must he have thought of me for blocking his way to the room where his youngsters slept?

My wife decided to visit the clinic. I had the kids tag along with her, and while they were out I scoured the room beside the gate. I hadn't been inside it in broad daylight since renting it out to the Kwŏns. As we had discovered when they moved in, their household possessions consisted entirely of their bedding and a few utensils for cooking and eating. Nothing unusual caught my eye. If there was anything that might afford me a clue, it would have to be his shoes.

In the very place where the cabinet or a similar piece of furniture should have been — the place for the most valuable household possession — there were nine pairs of shoes lined up like soldiers awaiting inspection. Six pairs were neatly polished; the remainder were covered with dust. Altogether, then, Kwŏn had owned ten pairs. It seems that he would select seven that suited his fancy, shine them all at once, and use them the following week, a different pair each day. While reflecting on the pair missing from the neatly shined group, I was struck by the realization that they would not return soon.

The time came for me to report Kwŏn's disappearance. It would be the first and last time I would notify Yi. I tried to remain as calm as possible as I called the policeman who had assured me time and again that I would one day grow to love my neighbor.

Translated by Bruce and Ju-chan Fulton

A Winter Commuter

Toward the end of the day Pak got a call at the publishers where he worked from Kim, who worked for a magazine. Kim was renowned among his friends for subduing his wife without fail in their quarrels with the snub that a woman without the charm of double eyelids should be ashamed even to exist, let alone to find fault with her husband.

"I just thought it's high time for all of us to have a confrontation."

Kim's voice sounded as bleak as a winter wind sweeping over a graveyard, and made the friendly jargon of "confrontation" as chilling as if it had come from a police officer. The gang had been calling their friendly get-togethers around liquor tables "confrontations" for some time now.

"A good idea!"

The thought of drinking is always pleasant. On a cold winter's day like this, the idea of tossing down a few cups of *sŏju* before the long ride home cannot but be alluring.

"It's a good idea, but...," Pak made haste to shake off the temptation which was tickling his throat mightily. "I've decided not to join your confrontations for the time being, unless there's some urgent business."

"Why, is your fountain pen leaking or something?"

"It's not that, but...."

Pak mumbled, ungallantly surveying the freckles on the accounting girl's face on the opposite side of the table. She was not double-lidded. The men in the editorial department had to come to the accounting office to make or receive phone calls, past the corridor by the president's office. Whenever there was a call for one of the men in the editorial office, this accounting girl sang out in a shrill voice, like a bus girl in the rush-hour. "Telephone for so-and-so!" It made the men most uncomfortable to tread the corridor past the president's office.

"Then, what can be your reason?"

Kim demanded in his flat, leaden voice.

"There are reasons. I'll tell you later."

"Ah! Sad! The great snowflakes touch no chords in us. When did we become scrap iron?"

Oh! Pak exclaimed to himself. His friend was talking about snow. Not just snow, but snow in big flakes. Pak looked out the window for the first time that afternoon. The accounting girl's innumerable freckles greeted his eyes first. But beyond the freckles was snow. Not ordinary snow, but snow in bountiful flakes, as large as the lumps of cottonwool hung onto Christmas trees. Pak exclaimed internally once again. Unbelievable!

The sky was clear blue when he had gone out this morning. The sun was quite warm for a winter's day at lunchtime when he had made a short trip to the nearby luncheonette. But snow had stolen down and covered the world while he was oblivious, hunting out misprinted and missing letters. He was taken by surprise, as when he found the prices of daily necessities had leaped to the heavens overnight. Well, it really was time they had a big snow. It was the twenty-second of December, just three days before Christmas.

"I'm sorry. You'll really have to excuse me."

The snow made him long for liquor all the more ardently. But it was clear that the more extraordinary the weather, the more haste he must make to return home. Well, maybe it was proof that he really was becoming scrap iron at just over thirty. The conversation was dragging. Freckled Miss Ch'oe's glance was much less amicable as she cast a look up at him. Pak was eager to conclude the talk.

"I really can't join you today. But I'll call you up during the New Year's holidays. Well, have a good time, and say hello for me to all!"

"You haven't forgotten that none of us can desert the gang and expect to live, have you? Traitor!"

The flat murmuring voice transmitted by the long wire sounded so sinister that Pak had a momentary illusion that Kim's habitual gloomy joke was some gangster's threat. The phone clicked off at the other end.

Pak was increasingly finding their friendly get-togethers burdensome. The expense was not such a great problem as they always gathered in a cheap dive and tossed down *sŏju*, but the problem was getting home after the party was over. The ride to Sŏngnam in the last bus just about did him in. Many of the passengers to Sŏngnam in the last bus were drunk, and they'd bicker over the fare with the bus girl, young enough to be their daughter. Arguments and quarrels began even before the bus started, and continued until they reached Sŏngnam. "Don't push!" "Ouch, you stepped on my feet!" "It's not me, it's the bus tumbling us all!" "If you don't like this crowd, you should take a taxi!" "Calm down everyone! We're all poor worms in this boat, so let's try to be charitable with one another!" "Shut up, you drunken bully, have you sopped up liquor through your ass?" "What does it matter to you how I take my liquor as long as I pay with my own money?" "Since when is it illegal for a working man to breathe before gentlemen in suits?" "Come on, you know it's no use arguing with a drunk. Just have a little patience, we're almost there!" These and many such abuses were tossed around while, on the other side of the bus, people in day-laborers' garb were fast asleep, unconscious of all the bustle. The sixty-odd minutes' ride amid the din and the smell of sweat and liquor always made Pak frightfully anxious. I must move to Seoul quickly and be rid of this hell, he couldn't help thinking. That's what he hated — the impatient hope that could find no support in reality.

The snow piled almost a foot high was soaking up the lights from shop windows like wet cottonwool. The Christmas trees and cards in the shop windows, blending with the high-piled snow, effused Christmas spirit. But the frozen road, made slick by the neighborhood urchins' sliding soles and covered with the continuously piling snow, was as dangerous as a well-camouflaged booby-trap. Pak, having walked down Chongro Street, now crossed the Ch'ŏnggye-ch'ŏn intersection. He kept walking toward the fifth avenue of Ŭlchiro, pushing and being pushed against the billowing pedestrians. The wall of one building, which looked as if determined to be a blot on the enlarged artery road, made the sidewalk look bent like a drawn bow. That wall, so very soiled and stinking so dreadfully with stale urine, gave one a sudden foul impulse. It was located exactly mid-way between the city bus and the express bus terminals.

It looked like there were more people waiting for buses than usual. There were long lines on both the city bus and the express bus sides. Pak, as usual, went over to the express bus side and attached himself to the tail end of the queue. In a little while his feet felt as stiff as frozen logs and the tips of his nose and ears felt numb as if they were detached from his flesh. Snow descended and made thick pads on his head and shoulders, but the long line was immovable.

A considerable time passed. The buses were running at much longer intervals. Cars went crawling over the roads, with heavy chains wound over the tires. It was understandable that buses would take longer to make the trip to and from Sŏngnam, as they had to traverse four or five steep hills. Since it was around the closing hour for offices, the queue fast grew a long tail behind Pak.

Against the possibility that he might have to wait still longer, Pak slipped into a nearby liquor stall and gulped down three cups of *sŏju* without any snack. The alcohol spread some warmth through his body but it didn't lighten his feelings. If it had been for something nice, a play, a sight-seeing tour, or to exchange a prize lottery ticket for cash, such a long wait might have been tolerable — even pleasant. But to have to stand in the snow on a dark winter street like a fish in the freezer just to go home to one's wife and children after a day's work was very unpleasant, to put it mildly.

It was eight o'clock already. Pak had been shivering and freezing there for an hour and a half. If he had known that this was what was going to happen, he would have joined his friends' "confrontation" and jabbered and giggled, and would have come for a late bus. He had been commuting from Sŏngnam to Seoul and back every day like a shuttlecock for many months now, but he had never been so anxious as today. Other city buses were running regularly, albeit slowly, but buses to Sŏngnam simply didn't appear. Pak gritted his teeth and resolved that he would get the hell out of Sŏngnam as quickly as....

Pak had settled in Sŏngnam shortly before it gained the status of a city, after having started as a settlement for those removed from illegal shacks which were torn down by government mandate. With great difficulty he had landed a position as a teacher of Korean in the new primary school there, with the help of one of his old teachers in his home town. He had resigned the hard-earned job for a reason that would look idiotic to anyone who had not been in his shoes. Anyway, as he had always walked to the primary school while he taught there, he had not realized that transportation to and from Seoul would be so excruciatingly exhausting. Moreover, this was the first winter he had commuted. And this was the first heavy snow since his residence in Sŏngnam. If it hadn't been, he would have been better prepared. He could at least have hardened himself mentally, like the others who have to depend on buses to commute long distances.

"Are we still only here?"

A strange young woman accosted him very naturally, coming up to his side. Pak, who could not imagine that the strange young woman could be talking to him, did not understand at first. But the woman's eyes were smiling at him. They were not double-lidded.

"Yes. Still here," he mumbled in confusion.

"Oh, brother! Still only here after two hours!" So saying, the girl stepped in between Pak and the man in front of him, with the most matter-of-fact expression on her face. "How can we do business in Seoul at this rate?"

It was only then that Pak understood. She was pretending to be his companion so she could jump the queue. Such impudent pluck that Pak could not condemn it. He rather thought it admirable.

As buses had virtually ceased, the long lines that stretched from Ch'ŏnggyech'ŏn to Ŭlchiro were in fact useless. But, since there was no telling how matters might develop, Pak asked the young woman to keep his place for him and once again went over to the liquor stall. There were many more customers than before, so he could not get a seat. Standing up, he tossed down three cups of *sŏju*. His capacity for liquor was really very modest. He only knew from experience that liquor was the best help for staying long in the cold open air. He felt dizzy at once. The liquor must have been too much for him on an empty stomach.

When he returned from the wine stall he found the queue much diminished and his place in it advanced much further towards the front. Many people had gotten out of line and were walking impatiently about the terminal. The advance was due, therefore, not to people having left on the bus but to people having given up.

Moving from where the queue started, a middle-aged man in a worn-out sweater was passing some message along the line in a loud voice. There was a stir among those who heard him. The stir spread very quickly along the queue.

"What is the man saying?" The young woman asked, looking back.

"I don't know. But it doesn't look like good news. Let's wait and see."

As the man came nearer, he could be heard distinctly.

"I'm sorry, ladies and gentlemen. I am sorry. We just got word from company headquarters..." The man in the sweater sneezed violently once, recovered his breath, and went on in a businesslike tone: "Because of the heavy snow on the road we are unable to operate our vehicles regularly. So, please do not rely on us any more, but look for other suitable ways of returning home."

The man repeated the same words over and over, as he moved down along the queue. "I am sorry, ladies and gentlemen. I am sorry."

A commotion began around Pak, too. A young man with long hair, standing right behind Pak, grumbled, "What do they mean, find other ways? Haven't they got the monopoly? Do they expect us to fly on wings, or what? Motherfuckers!"

"Then why didn't you let us know earlier? How do you expect us to find other ways at this hour, and frozen stiff like this?" A woman's shrill, infuriated voice shot up from somewhere further down the queue. Every protest was followed by the stony voice of the man repeating, like something played on an old gramophone hollowly shaking in the cold night air: "I'm sorry. I am very sorry. The condition of the roads does not permit...We will do our best...I am sorry. So sorry."

"Fuck you! Do apologies mend anything?"

"What's going to become of us?" The young woman in front of him fretted in a fear-strained voice. "How can we go home if the buses have stopped?"

To reassure himself, Pak needed to reassure her. So he began by telling her not to worry. Is it likely that this many people would freeze to death in the middle of the capital city? he said. He told her that the authorities would certainly think of some way to transport them home. But, as if lacking confidence in his own words, he kept glancing toward the taxi stand. No salvation could be hoped for from that quarter. As soon as a taxi came into view, sturdy young men rushed toward it in a body, pushing each other like angry bulls. A weakling like himself was sure to be trodden down flat before even joining the swarm. Where rough strength decides, it was best that he did not think of trying his luck. With inward abandon, Pak gave himself up to the flow of time.

It was already past ten o'clock. From somewhere in the distance, music from the radio let loose by a loudspeaker floated on. A woman announcer's calm voice followed, reminding teenagers it was late in the evening and that evil allurements of the night streets could best be avoided by returning to the homes where their parents were waiting for them.

It was not that buses had ceased altogether. One or two buses appeared at intervals of what seemed like eternity and made people fret and stamp. When a bus marked with the familiar line number crawled toward them, like a joke or a chance mistake, an amazing horde rushed to it instantly, and all hell broke loose. Arguments and fist fights arose, people fell down and were trodden on, and some climbed into the bus through the windows. Those who had been standing in line like model citizens cursed the shameless horde and threw snowballs at them. There were several policemen from the nearby police box on patrol, but they could do nothing to put to order an agitated crowd of thousands. Then buses stopped altogether. Naturally, there was an end to the sport of snowball throwing.

Pak asked the girl once more to keep watch over his place and made a brief visit to a tearoom to warm himself. The girl also asked Pak to keep watch over her place and returned, blushing, after a brief absence. It must have been a long-withheld trip to the toilet. Some of the sturdy young men took the company official's advice and left, in threes and fives, singing pop songs like marching tunes. They were going to go to the edge of the city by other city buses and then walk to Sŏngnam. They were reckoning that if they walked briskly they would reach Sŏngnam by curfew time. But most of the others, whether from the fear of walking a good couple of hours in knee-deep snow, or from thinking it was too early to give up hope of salvation altogether, just cast well-wishing and anxious glances at the young men's backs. Now that there was no guarantee of any means of transportation home, standing in line was meaningless. But the queue didn't disperse; it persisted, in the midst of the restless and amorphous crowd, in the naive belief that should salvation come from somewhere, somehow, the priority of the queue would be respected. Pak was among the literal-minded people. His jaw ached and his shoulder blades were stiff from standing there trembling too long. His upper and lower teeth chattered, beating plaintive time. His body inside his coat was shrivelled up like a chrysalis in a cocoon. The snowflakes had ceased, but the wind that swept up and scattered powdery dry snow stung the exposed skin like porcupines gone berserk. The *sŏju*, which he felt when drinking it was a little excessive, lost potency before the merciless cold and made its effect felt briefly around the eyes and on the tip of the tongue before disappearing altogether. Pak chuckled to himself, recalling how his dreams of the night before were tranquilly fanciful, giving no hint of such tribulations to follow.

"Any girls here like to follow me to a cozy inn?"

Long-haired youths in blue jeans slouched up to girls and twanged the invitation. It made everyone realize that they ought to prepare against the possibility of being unable to get home. Indeed, it almost looked hopeless now.

"Any girl is welcome, squint-eyed or button-nosed. You there, why not have some fun, free? We'll both come out winners!"

Around the corner a group of four or five girls were standing, sobbing fretfully. Drunken youths were shuffling around them, trying to get them to listen to their insolent offers.

"Er...Excuse me, mister!"

The girl in front of him addressed him in crisp, ringing tones, looking into his eyes.

"Er...What will you do if you can't go back home tonight?"

"Well I...I don't know."

The girl took a deep breath, like a diving champion on the spring-board. Then she asked with the look of one plunging into a pool: "You're planning to sleep in an inn, aren't you? Aren't you?"

The girl straightened herself and collected her breath, like a diver who had plunged deep and gained the surface again: "Oh, how nice! I'd like to ask a favor of you. Please take me with you."

Even though Pak's answer had not been definite, the girl had interpreted it to suit herself and made her astonishing request. Her voice was most inappropriately high for a request of that nature. Sure enough, people within hearing distance turned interested glances towards the two. If it had been in some other place or circumstance, any man this side of ninety would have been dazed and excited. But, in that place and situation, Pak was only embarrassed, and didn't know where to look.

"I promise I won't bother you. Just let me sleep curled up in a corner. And I'll repay you for your kindness. I promise I will. Please, please take me with you."

The girl entreated, like one determined not to give up. Pak's attention was turned off for the first time from the problem of obtaining transportation home, and he began to study the girl with interest. She was very small, too small even, for a woman. She looked about twenty, but, instead of blooming as a girl her age ought to do, she was thin to the point of emaciation, and the rough, thick coat that hung loosely on her looked as oppressive as a raincoat on a pullet. There was no trace whatever of make-up on her face, and it wasn't a notable face in any way, but the features were pleasing and regular. However, the thick coat of poverty which was spread over her entire face stifled the attraction that should have shown there. She looked like a plant that had been eaten away from infancy by a burrowing worm. Pak had a momentary delusion of looking at an illustrated exposition of how poverty eats up a woman's beauty and can turn her into a sinister hag. Then it occurred to him that it was his own portrait he was looking at in the girl's form. Pak also felt that if he had ever tinkered with dissipation he would by now be struggling in the swamp of repentance and guilt.

"But why d'you ask such a favor of me, of all people?"

It wasn't that he was going to refuse her request. He always carried enough money for a night's lodging at an inn in case of emergencies. A double room would cost only slightly more than a single. He could even get a separate room for the girl. Therefore, it was just that he wanted to know why she picked him, of all the crowd there, to make such a dangerous request. It was partly an expression of his admiration for her boldness.

"I've had to live most of my life on my wits alone. So, even though I'm still young I can tell people quite accurately by looking at them. As soon as I set eyes on you I knew you were a kind-hearted and honorable sort of person."

Oh yeah? Pak exclaimed to himself. He smiled involuntarily. How many men would there be, who would behave only "honorably" when taking a girl to an inn at her own request? Not very many, it's likely. If it was not meant to be an empty compliment, the girl was telling him that he looked like a "safe" partner in a risky adventure. Then, not being a saint or a fool, should he feel flattered or insulted at such an assessment of him coming from a girl?

Unconscious of what went on in Pak's mind, the girl was celebrating her luck. Pak gazed with wonder at the mouth of the girl chattering on, completely unmindful of the many eyes turned on her. It was her voice, and her voice only, that bore witness to her youth. It was a clear voice, frail but also resonant. The agile and youthful impression she gave off was owing really to her vivacious tone, so unlike her shabby appearance. She was chattering and laughing incessantly. But perhaps it was only her stubbornness and tenacity that made her control her trembling body with forced gaiety. It was likely that she, like him, had not had dinner yet. There was little likelihood of rescue in sight. Pak grabbed the girl's arm and headed toward the tearoom, not caring whether people around them thought him a profligate or not.

"Surely, doomsday is nigh. What kind of a world is this in which girls lure men to bed?"

As he had feared, lament and chuckling from behind hit the back of his head.

"Some guys are lucky, even on days like this!"

Pak prayed that those words would freeze in the air before reaching the girl's ears. But, unless her hearing was impaired, there was no way she could have escaped hearing them.

"May I have your orders?" The waitress asked.

The girl hesitated a little and ordered coffee. Pak ordered tea mixed with wine. And he also ordered a boiled egg for each of them.

"Get out! Go away!" The waitress was yelling at someone. The tearoom was as crowded as a seething stew pot. "Do you think this is a waiting room at a train station? Go away at once!"

The tearoom was simmering incessantly with customers seated to full capacity, customers waiting for seats to become available, thick cigarette smoke, blaring music from loudspeakers, and innumerable voices straining to be heard over the music and noise. It was lucky that they could grab seats soon after coming into the tearoom. Tearooms closed early, in compliance with the energy-saving policy in the wake of the oil crisis, but this tearoom was open late for the late commuters to Sŏngnam.

"We're going to order something! Look, I've got money!" An elderly couple was arguing with the waitress. The couple looked like country folks inexperienced in places like tearooms, and it was most likely that they drifted into the tearoom not to have tea but to escape from the cold, like sparrows chased by an icy blizzard. They eyed the waitress and the customers with fearful eyes and moved from beside one stove to another. The waitress, even in that turmoil, could tell paying and free-riding customers apart with unerring instinct, and chased out loungers with shrill irritation.

"All right, then. Place your orders. What'll they be?"

"God! Do you mean for us to drink tea standing up? We'll order drinks when we get seats and collect our breaths a little."

"Do you think I'll be fooled? We don't want your orders. Just get out of here at once!"

"For shame, young woman! How can you treat two elderly folks like us as if we were a couple of beggars?"

"How can we do business, if you two keep standing here blocking the passage and sucking up warmth?"

"Stop this pushing! Don't you have an aged father and mother?"

The elderly man was responding to the waitress with exaggerated naivety. She was as evil-tempered as a crossed witch, without the compensating charm of double-lidded eyes. Pak grinned when his thoughts reached the double-lidded part. Then, the face of the girl, who had been waiting demurely beside him for the order to arrive, became distorted.

"I promise I'd repay you for your kindness," she pronounced decisively. "Didn't I tell you I'll repay you for your kindness? If you think I'm such a...such a girl, I'm awfully hurt."

"Oh, I er...You misunderstood."

"You must understand that what I asked you didn't...didn't come out easily. I might have looked like one who can say such things casually, but it really needed desperate courage."

"You really have misunderstood. What I was amused at was this. I have a friend by the name of Kim who..." Pak explained about Kim's adroitness in subduing his wife by reference to her handicap of lacking double eyelids.

"Are you married, too?"

Pak told her that he had a wife and a one-year-old boy, and that, though his wife also lacked double-lidded charm, he didn't snub her for it like his friend. The girl giggled excitedly, and looked at the waitress walking toward the counter. The waitress had given up, and the elderly couple had won.

"There's nothing better than a stove in this kind of weather. Though we did have some harsh words from that girl young enough to be our daughter, it's much better than freezing stiff outside."

"Of course it is."

The elderly woman, who had been tongue-tied till now, standing like a shy girl, chimed in at once. The old man's face shone with triumph, like one who had just vanquished a formidable foe, and his wife's eyes were overflowing with pride and reliance on the solid strength of her spouse.

The young couple sitting across the table from Pak and the girl had been casting suspicious glances at the newcomers. Their faces showed rather too obviously the displeasure of having their privacy invaded, and their postures expressed their determination to defend their happiness with bodily strength, if necessary. They were talking almost in whispers.

Their orders arrived. While the waitress disbursed the contents of her tray on the table, the girl beside Pak lifted her purse and placed it on her knees. It was a sturdy, pragmatic purse, somewhat like a student's.

"Are you a student?" Pak asked.

He studied her face self-consciously, wishing that his voice hadn't sounded as if he wished she was not. But her voice, as she answered, was completely light.

"Ye-es. That is, I'm a student twice a day. It saves me twenty *won* in the way of bus fare."

She smiled brightly, as if to say she didn't regard the deceit as a great crime. Her big purse, the one book in her hand, the beige woolen mittens, plus the short hair, the frugal, almost shabby attire, the presumed self-confidence of her manner and tone — all these bore witness to her effort to look like a student. Sipping the warm coffee, she talked to him about herself. Pak had never seen anyone who relished a cup of coffee so ecstatically as she did. Holding it in both her cupped hands, she sipped from it in little sips, slowly, and looked as if she thanked all the world for that bounty. Pak was amused. He listened to her with a warm patronizing smile, and encouraged her now and then with a word or two. He felt smugly towards her. It was a superiority of the kind that express bus riders feel towards riders of city buses. The feeling was aroused not so much because he was at the moment doing a small kindness to a young woman many years his junior; it was the kind of superiority he felt towards most inhabitants of Sŏngnam city most of the time.

"I guess you work in Seoul?" the girl asked.

"Yes. I work for a small publishing firm."

Pak did not, of course, let out that he had once been a schoolteacher in Sŏngnam. If the girl shared the inordinate respect for schoolteachers with other inhabitants of Sŏngnam, he would have to explain at length why he had quit that enviable position. And there was little likelihood of his explanation being comprehensible to her. How can people who deem white-collar workers' lot to be a blessing little short of Elysium understand quitting a teaching post in protest against the private school owner's greed and despotism?

"How long have you been living in Sŏngnam?"

"A little less than a year. I came to know there was such a city for the first time when the papers reported the settlers' protest disturbances. I never imagined I'd be having anything to do with the place. But strange chances take one..."

"Shame on you, for shame!"

"What?"

"You sound as if you are ashamed of living in Sŏngnam."

Pak felt stripped naked. He tried to cover up his shameful secret before the young girl with a smile and a joke: "Well, you sound as if you are awfuly proud of living in Sŏngnam."

"Yes, I am. I am proud. I always tell everyone proudly that I live in Sŏngnam. My family had been wandering from city to city until we came to Sŏngnam. So I have a home town now, for the first time in my life. What does it matter how late in life I came by it or who gave it to me? As the popular song has it, home is where you belong. So, Sŏngnam is precious to me. More so I suppose than to most others."

Pak was lost for a rejoinder.

"Oh, I almost forgot. My name's Yong-sun. Family name, Chŏng. It's a too-common name."

"Pleased to meet you. I'm Pak."

"I hope more and more people like you will come to live in Sŏngnam."

"Yes? Why?"

"So that Sŏngnam will become a more cultured and decent city."

Pak broke out laughing. The young couple across the table also broke out laughing. Though pretending to ignore their presence, the couple had in fact been listening with interest to the talk between Pak and the girl. It was natural that they aroused curiosity. Miss Chŏng looked cross.

"It's no laughing matter. Although not many people are aware of it, many famous people live in Sŏngnam. Yi Tae-yŏp, for example, and..."

"You mean the actor Yi Tae-yŏp?"

"Yes. He and other actors and singers and TV personalities...."

She was a very exceptional case. Although Pak had met quite a number of the inhabitants of Sŏngnam, he had never met anyone so proud of his dwelling-place as Miss Chŏng. She went on to recite the new developments and improvements in Sŏngnam City, just as if she had been the city's spokesperson.

Pak did not share her enthusiasm in the least. He hated being asked where he lived. People, when they found out that he lived in Sŏngnam, looked at him with sudden curiosity, wondering how he happened to be living in such a notorious place. Or maybe he just thought they looked at him with curiosity, because of his inferiority complex concerning the place. At any rate, he always hastened to add that he had moved there only very recently. Of course he despised himself for it, but that despicable defense had become an inveterate habit. And Pak was not the only one with such a practice. Perhaps because the incident of massive protest still cast a painful shadow, people placed very great importance on the time of their moving into the city. The indigenous population of the area emphasized that they were natives of the city, as if the word "native" had no taint of backwardness and barbarity, but was a gilded word denoting pride and prestige. The "natives" affirmed, whenever there was a chance, that they were descendants of the landowning scholar-literati of the Kyŏnggi-do area, and that they were therefore to be distinguished from the settlers. And the newcomers, though they had less to assert in the way of inherited prestige, also wanted to be distinguished from the settlers as much as the ''natives.''

''What's there to be ashamed of in honestly struggling to live?'' she said, and, perhaps judging that they were quite friends by now, began telling him about her own life. Although the first impression she gave was of poverty and gloom, she was talkative. And she knew how to talk without being boring. But the interest owed mostly to her manner, not to the content of her talk. Hers was just another typical settler's family. Plenty of misfortunes and failures, plus a lot of tears, some verbal pride, but deep unhealed wounds and several unfulfillable wishes. All these were to be glimpsed between pauses in her monologue.

''I'm learning Japanese at an institute now.''

Pak noted for the first time that the book lying on her purse was a Japanese reader of the semi-advanced level.

''I quit high school the year before last and jumped into the struggle for existence. Well, 'struggle for existence' sounds rather hackneyed. Anyway, I've done most anything that a girl could do. Wigs, stuffed toys, machine embroidery, you name it, I've done it. But, whatever it was, it tired me out and gave me next to nothing to take home. I made a little calculation one day on a torn piece of paper. It said eighteen years. Eighteen, no less! I would have to keep at it for no less than eighteen years to attain my goal! Think of it. To go on for eighteen more years, scrimping like this! Then I'll by thirty-seven. I cried, because it was too unfair. I cried my heart out and I quit the factory. I enrolled at the Japanese institute the next day."

As when she had asked him to take her along to an inn, her voice was high and nervous and made heads turn, even in the midst of the thick noise. The couple across the table had put down their defenses altogether and were listening with undisguised interest. Pak felt very uncomfortable to be enclosed by curiosity on all sides, but there was no way he could stem the tide of her loquacity. The girl seemed completely unconscious of the many eyes upon her and went on in her excited manner. Or perhaps she was conscious of the glances but did not care.

"Don't misunderstand. Not all girls who learn Japanese do so from dishonorable motives. They say that even in a lion's den one can live if one has all one's wits about. I know that I'm not likely to come by any big money. But who knows, the Japanese come over with sacks of money to invest; why shouldn't I hit upon some ingenious way of assisting them and get a share of the profit? In only about a month I'll be getting my diploma. Then I'm going to apply for a tourist guide's position."

Beneath her shabby and undernourished exterior there breathed a healthy, animal instinct. She had, hidden somewhere in her, canine teeth and claws sharp and powerful enough to scratch and bite any antagonist, as sharp and powerful as those of primitive man in nomadic days. She betrayed the obsession and dedication of those who cling to one thing as a last resort and as compensation for everything else. They certainly were blessed assets that she had, something not everyone can acquire by wishing and trying.

With the thawing of his frozen body came weariness. He felt tired out like one who has been beaten up and then laid to rest. The warmth of the tearoom was most snug. It felt almost as if they were sealed in by a vacuum from the cold and the darkness and the noise of outside. The anxiety of the queuing crowds felt like a far-away affair that had nothing to do with him. He almost felt like a tourist from the civilized world come to watch the agitation and discomfiture of a primitive tribe. The liquor which had been stricken impotent by the cold now spread throughout his entire body and engulfed him in a pleasantly tingling sensation. The girl seemed as intoxicated as Pak. Although she had not touched liquor, she was more excited and elated than Pak, who had tossed down a total of six cups of *sŏju*. With the release of the tide of words that had been dammed up in her heart, her face shone red with excitement. The almost abnormal flush made her so gorgeous that Pak felt like calling on all the world to behold her beauty. She was blooming like a nubile girl of twenty ought to be.

But, for some reason, the flush on Miss Chŏng began to fade after a short spell of silence. Then the flush vanished completely from her cheeks and in its place spread waves of ashen-grey sorrow. Her figure relapsed into that of a plant whose growth has been undermined and arrested in infancy. She was shaking violently. The transformation was painful to watch. Pak felt as if he had just witnessed the blooming and fading of the cactus flower which blooms only once in its life, briefly. Her voice, when she spoke again, was not the high and lively voice of a young woman full of plans, but was sunken and despondent like an asthmatic old woman's.

"I must tell you the truth. I've been lying."

Her voice was as shaky as her body. "It's a lie that I love Sŏngnam. And I'm not proud to be its inhabitant at all. It's not my home town or anything. It's just an alien place to me and always will be. Papa still thinks that Seoul has ruined him and then kicked him out. He can't get rid of the shock of the day our shack was smashed down by the bulldozer. So he's still yearning for the day he can return to Seoul like a triumphant general and live like a prince, bullying all his neighbors. But I don't blame him. Far from it. I'd like to help him. I'd do anything to help make his dream come true. I'll make money and make his dream come true. To move back to Seoul is my dream, too. I'm sure it's a dream for most anyone like us. The people outside were blaming the weather bureau, the bus company, the road and transportation authorities, and so on. But really, they wouldn't be in such a plight it they had been more clever and could afford a house in Seoul. If they lived in Seoul, they would have nothing to worry about even if snow piled two yards high and buried all the houses."

Pak felt as if he had been pushed down a high precipice. It was also a feeling of betrayal. Fury began to seethe in him, for no clear-cut reason he could name. In the twinkling of an eye the fury changed into a crude sexual desire. It was, in fact, the sadistic urge one felt before a much-trodden worm still struggling for life. He felt like crushing the young woman and extinguishing her breath once and for all. It was an astonishing and senseless state of mind. But the urge was so irresistible that he was afraid he would go berserk if he didn't gratify it at once. He decided to force himself upon her.

"Let's get moving!" he said hoarsely. Grabbing a wrist of the girl, who was surprised and cringing before his sudden fierceness, Pak hurriedly paid the bill and almost dragged her out of the tearoom.

It was just as cold outside as before. Or rather, it felt much colder than before they had warmed themselves. Miss Chŏng's skinny wrist was trembling. The skin of the wrist was rough, and Pak felt as if he could feel the thick gooseflesh through the sleeve of her underwear. He did not feel in the least guilty. He was only dimly conscious of the responsibility attendant on such an act, and was thinking up excuses with a part of his mind. I can't be held responsible, he was telling himself as he emerged into the road dragging Miss Chŏng. The *sŏju* drunk on an empty stomach is to blame. And the unexpected snow. If someone has to be held responsible, then it can only be my creator.

"You hear that?" Miss Chŏng asked with her tired-out voice, panting for breath.

"Yes."

Christmas carols drifted towards them, blown on gusts of wind. It must be a courtesy extended by the record shop.

"They're celebrating the birth of the infant Christ."

"Oh...that's *Hallelujah*."

"And the one before was *The Red-Nosed Reindeer*."

"What does it matter if it's red-nosed or black-nosed? Well, anyway, I wish you a Merry Christmas, though it's still three days off."

"Merry Christmas to you, too," said Miss Chŏng, with a rather uneasy smile.

Around the terminal it was even more chaotic than before. Several thousand whose return to lair had been interrupted were swarming in the street on the freezing winter night. A number of police troopers who had arrived in a truck were trying hard to keep the swarm orderly. The only "development" that had taken place in the meantime was that the crowd's sorrow and loneliness had become illuminated. A host of newspaper company cars had arrived and cameramen were flashing lights on the crowd and clicking away, standing on the hoods and roofs of their vehicles. Every time a flash exploded, people waved and shouted, desperately trying to get their presence advertized. It looked so comic that a foreigner who chanced by might have thought that it was some mass recreation or other.

"It's no use standing in this cold any more. It's hopeless. Let's take shelter in a warm hotel room and get some sleep."

Pak tugged at Miss Chŏng's sleeve impatiently. Miss Chŏng was hesitant, and looked as if she would like to wait a bit and see if there'd be the least possibility; still she also seemed not unattracted to the idea of a warm shelter. But an unexpected hindrance presented itself. Pak's design was completely shattered by the hindrance — or salvation — that appeared right at the decisive moment. A police patrol car began to drive around, announcing through its loudspeaker: "Dear citizens of Sŏngnam. We are so very sorry you have been inconvenienced in this cold weather. But please set your minds at ease now. In a little while emergency coaches will arrive to take you all safely back to your homes. We understand you are cold and tired, but please be orderly, as befits democratic citizens. Please don't worry any more, it will be but a short while.''

It was after midnight that the emergency coaches arrived, more than a dozen at once. Great chaos and confusion arose once again. Even in that chaos, Miss Chŏng moved nimbly, exhibiting unsuspected strength.

"I'll get on one and secure a place for you, too!"

Perhaps she thought that it was a good chance to repay him for his little treat. Anyway, leaving that shouted declaration behind, she plunged fearlessly into the great whirlwind of the pushing and shoving crowd. It was so instantaneous that Pak did not have a chance to get hold of her and keep her back.

The great human whirlwind swallowed up her frail form in no time. A few desperate wails shook the night air, and a number of the people who had been rushing toward the buses fell forward. It happened in the twinkling of an eye. Police ran in, waved away people, and pulled up those who had fallen down. Pak rushed there, too, and pulled up Miss Chŏng. But she fell down again when he slackened his support. She was unconscious.

"Wake up, Miss Chŏng! Wake up!"

Pak shook her a couple of times. There was no response.

"She seems badly hurt. Maybe she should be taken to a hospital," someone said in a flat, emotionless voice. "Do you know her?"

Pak turned his eyes. A young man's face under a police cap came into view. Realizing that it was a policeman, Pak came to his senses, as if he had had a bucketful of cold water thrown over him. He realized all too clearly the implications of the situation he was in. The steps he would have to take, the responsibilities he would be under, and other incidental encumbrances quickly flashed through his head. Instantly Pak became a very practical human being.

"You mean me?" Straightening up, he spoke like one just awakened from sleep. "No. I don't know her at all. She had been standing in line in front of me till just now. It's a pity. A great pity," Pak said hurriedly and moved off to a distance.

The buses were being delayed in starting because of Miss Chŏng. Everybody else who had fallen down was only slightly hurt and got on buses with the help of other people. Only Miss Chŏng still lay on the ground, unconscious. The terminal looked desolate, the enormous crowd having almost all gotten on one bus or another. Only a few people still lingered on, out of excessive curiosity. Pak, after remaining quite some time outside the ring of spectators, began to walk slowly toward one of the buses. Then he heard a sobbing from behind. Miss Chŏng must have awakened.

"Please, please don't take me to a hospital. We don't have that kind of money, and my family can't go on without me. Please, just let me go. I'm all right."

After a little more delay, the buses took off one after another. The tribulations of many hours were finally at an end. The passengers, whether seated or standing, began to doze, almost to a person. But Pak did not feel sleepy. He tried very hard to cancel out all thought of Miss Chŏng — not only worries about her injured state, but all thoughts about what had happened between them. He told himself that Miss Chŏng was no Christ. His denying her could not be compared to Peter's denial of Jesus before the Romans.

The buses stopped in front of the Sŏngnam city police station. A woman who had slept all the way there exclaimed, "Oh, it has snowed!" as if she had not been hideously inconvenienced by it already. Pak sneezed violently a few times, as if in response to her. Cold must be gripping him now that he was beginning to feel easy. Passing the sleepy crowd with quick steps, Pak diligently trod the silent streets. But he stopped short when a voice called, "Excuse me!" He pulled up like one grabbed by the collar from behind, and made an about-face. Miss Chŏng was smiling at him with all her might from the distance. Pak went up to her and quickly studied her eyes. There was not a hint of blame, and they were as calm and clear as undisturbed lake water.

"Thank you for the coffee, and the egg."

"Are you hurt badly?"

"No. Well, I'll have to say good-bye now. I go this way."

"Allow me to walk you home."

"No. I'm quite all right. Well, *sayonara*."

Miss Chŏng mustered up another smile at him and walked away into the white night, leaving unsteady footprints on the snow. Pak murmured low toward her receding back: "Good-bye, Yong-sun!"

Pak stood on the spot under the mercurial lamp like a statue until Miss Chŏng disappeared completely from sight. The thick snow had enveloped Sŏngnam completely, like heavy armor. The black ditch, sooty with waste and the dregs from the coal mine, the innumerable shacks and shanties clinging to the slopes of the hills like scabs on a bad skin sore, and all the numerous husbands and wives and children sleeping in such shabby dwellings — all were covered white, purified by the bountiful snow. Amid such purity, Pak didn't know where to turn his eyes and stood like one ashamed and guilty before all the world.

Translated by Suh Ji-moon

Gang Beating

These days we often see people show more courtesy toward a container than its contents. So I feel it necessary to describe to you in detail a certain building before its people. In short, the staff and customers who come here—regardless of their social standing, age or sex—are nothing more than accessories to the building, ornaments at best.

Those who are in a position to know the building, all know this well.

The building in question occupied an awkward and indecisive site — that is, neither at the center nor on the outskirts of the city.

The structure was so dilapidated that the city government, on the grounds that it defiled the appearance of the street, had three times issued repair orders under a time limit, with the full, nauseatingly full, knowledge that a building with that great a degree of wear must have an equally long history.

Indeed it had admirably weathered a long period of time. It had passed through all sorts of unusual trials amid all sorts of hostile people. It had also had to contend with the power of nature, which had begun to eat into its very foundation. Yet there was no end to its sorry lot: the building had become involved in a lawsuit.

When the repair order had been disobeyed and the time limit set by the city passed, the authorities had shown their indignation by issuing another order, this time for evacuation. But the dissatisfied owner of the building had brought the matter before the court.

The order was of course lawful. But the reasons for issuing it would have been more convincing had they been couched in terms that lives might be lost.

Right across the street from the building was a fire station. It was so close that you could see the young fireman stationed in the lookout, whiling away the long summer afternoons scratching his thighs with a carefree air.

As though measuring themselves against the fire station lookout, a few other buildings rose one after another beside this one, and the alley running between led to an agricultural machinery factory.

The factory was pitifully primitive; they manufactured sprayers and the like by sheer physical strength, by hammering iron plates this way or that.

The factory adjoined the two-storey building, on the ground floor of which was a cheap inn. Next to it was a newly-built inner wing which had been added to a hospital.

Most of those who passed in front of the hospital gate would find their attention caught by something that made them feel uneasy, and would look back over their shoulders. Then they would soon find what had bothered them — the upstairs floor of the two-storey building with its shabby walls and windows, held up insecurely by the cheap inn downstairs. Its shabbiness was so glaring even a nearsighted man could detect it. Those with better vision could locate the sign and read it.

Old as it was, it was, nonetheless, a building all right. And so, like other buildings, it had walls.

Originally these had been lime-plastered with patterns of raised waves on them created by letting kneaded lime flow down on the surfaces of the walls long enough for them to dry, and then applying pink paint to show them to their best advantage.

However, time had played havoc with them; the plaster and the paint had come off in such a "democratically" disordered fashion that they reminded you of the sloppy, streaked face of a hard-living woman as she got out of bed late in the morning.

Of the four walls, the one facing the street attracted the most notice. It had a small window in its upper part with four panes, each of which bore one of four characters in gold leaf, "san", "ho", "ta", and "bang", which, put together in that order, meant Sanho Tearoom. This was the most dignified part of the whole building.

This window could either perform its original duty as a window, or serve as a signboard, according to the way it was opened.

Usually it remained shut, but when somebody happened to open the right side to the left, those passing below would see the letters so arranged as to read either "san" and "ta" or "ho" and "bang". Though this was the only means with which the place advertized its existence, nobody in the city could mistake it for anything else.

Now that you have seen the outer appearance of the building, try to visualize the inside.

From the entryway, it would be better for you to walk forward with quick steps, not turning to the right, because the toilet there, used by the people of the tearoom and the downstairs inn alike, irrespective of sex, would spoil your visit from the outset, whether or not its door was open.

Past the toilet, the stairs would immediately come into sight. Exactly twenty-seven wooden steps going straight up, steep ones with no landings. Thanks to this stupidity of design, you would, if you were in the company of a woman, soon be enjoying the knight's role, with no need for preparation.

The worn-out steps would creak more loudly the higher you climbed, until finally you would be seized with fear, such as is experienced by someone seriously ill who is being led into an operating theater and who doubts whether or not he will return alive to the bright world.

At the head of the stairs, you would unexpectedly find your other self. He would have arrived in advance to welcome you as you ascended the steps. He would look larger or even fatter than you or grotesquely uglier because parts of his face would be distorted.

However, you would not have to bother yourself with him, nothing but the playful product of a full-length mirror hanging on the wall.

Then note the letters inscribed on the upper and lower parts of the looking glass. The ones above read: "Congratulations on your progress," while those on the lower part: "The members of the Seventh Full Moon Viewing Association of Yŏngsaeng Girls' High School."

The looking glass, its originally uneven surface looking all the patchier because the mercury coating on its back had peeled off in places, befitted the general atmosphere of the place as well as the customers. It did not stare at them as they came trudging up the creaky steps out of breath, nor did it remind them of what they really looked like.

Now at last you may enter. A pull on the doorknob beside the mirror will be enough to allow you to become a member of the Sanho family. At first you will find yourself in complete darkness like that of a cave. Then, in the darkness, you will see two neat rows of teeth, like so many porcelain chips, smiling white. This smile will unhesitatingly draw you into the tearoom.

1

On this day too, things were the way they used to be. Son, the proprietress of the teahouse, greeted Kim Shi-ch'ŏl, a country primary school teacher, with those white teeth of hers and her usual white smile as he entered.

In the course of the usual greetings he exchanged with the proprietress at the counter, the darkness that had stood like a barrier before him gradually gave way to the chairs arranged in rows in the room. One row after another, the chairs in turn began to occupy space as the darkness subsided.

As he had expected, the second chair from the right corner, from which Kim Shi-ch'ŏl could see the fire station lookout whenever he opened the window beside it, was not occupied. Or, to be more precise, it was so arranged by the proprietress as not to be occupied.

Kim Shi-ch'ŏl dumped himself into the chair he

was accustomed to sitting in.

"Well, you went to work with your letter of resignation still in your pocket today, didn't you?" Son asked, as she sat opposite him. A woman who still had some years before she reached fifty, with that fleshiness often seen in women of her age, Son gave the impression of having grown old gracefully, so that she had gained for herself the nickname of Maitreya Bodhisattva, the merciful Buddha.

"You're well aware of that, aren't you?" Kim Shi-ch'ŏl answered bluntly.

The chair in which Kim was sitting was an old-fashioned wooden one, with a low seat and arms a bit too high, so that whenever he sat in it, he was forced to present an arrogant-looking posture ill-befitting a country primary school teacher.

"You haven't had any good opportunities?" Son asked.

"Lots of opportunities. I'm a mere primary school teacher. I can quit any time. It's not because I don't have any opportunities, but because I'm not sharp enough to quit. You know all that, don't you?"

"You have been patient enough. So, be a little more patient. They say they are going to raise teachers' salaries. Then you'll be in easier circumstances."

"Does salary matter much? What matters is social status, that is, the points they usually give a primary school teacher when they consider him as a prospective son-in-law or bridegroom."

"Take it easy. What you need first is rest, I'm sure. Have a nap, as you would in your own room," the woman said. Then she left. She knows the right moment to leave, Kim thought. The voice of the woman rang in his ear as crisply as though he were eating a slice of pear.

Kim Shi-ch'ŏl slept for some time and awoke to find the agricultural machinery factory below had gotten down to work. They were busy beating away at iron plates, making a great noise. And, along with this noise, came Son's voice.

"Everybody thinks so at first, but soon you make nothing of it. You soon get used to noises that come regularly." Son was talking to a couple of stray customers who had dropped in knowing nothing about her establishment. However, their grumblings continued.

"What a nasty tearoom this is. Look at those lamps and decorations. They are all stupid."

"Didn't I tell you so? How about the music? Anyway, a nineteenth century product, this place is."

This sort of comment was, of course, a blow to Son, who thought of herself as a humble fixture of Sanho Tearoom.

Nevertheless, in a calm voice and with a broad, Buddha-like smile on her face she began to prevail upon the young couple to understand her ideas. "Light accompanies shade. Of course, the former is better than the latter. But light alone won't do, since it only makes man tired, feel parched. It's normal for shade to follow light. Particularly in a city. In this sense Sanho Tearoom serves as a shade, the only shade left in our city today. Those who are oppressed by the burning sun of life drag their tired feet here, seeking rest. Formalities or keeping up appearances have nothing to do with this place. Nobody finds fault with those who do things a little out of the ordinary. Gentlemanly clothes are unnecessary. Work clothes are better for rolling in a grassy field.''

This was the belief she firmly held, armed with which she had defended Sanho through half her life. Because of this belief she had experienced many difficulties. But it was also because of this belief that she was able to maintain Sanho as it stood today.

She never thought of her teahouse operation as a business. To her, it was social work for those shabby failures who sought shade in which to rest, like chicks seeking the wing of a hen. And she satisfied herself with the thought that she was that hen.

''You want coffee?'' Kim Shi-ch'ŏl heard Miss Hyŏn, the waitress, ask the couple. Her voice sounded quarrelsome. She had a habit of glancing downward with her chin up when she talked. Several times Son had told Miss Hyŏn to get rid of the habit, but to no avail; this habit of hers was born of her disrespect for the customers.

''What do you want?'' the woman asked the man.

''Coffee,'' the man answered.

''One coffee and one tomato juice,'' the woman said tersely.

Miss Hyŏn turned and left, swinging her hips the length of the aisle.

''You ordered tomato juice?'' Son asked with a look of surprise.

''Yes. Anything wrong?''

''Of course not. Tomato juice? Yes, it is good for cultivating a woman's beauty. And — ''

Then, Son went on in a persuasive tone. ''But, of all drinks, coffee is best. Don't you agree? Moreover, what we Sanho people serve customers with confidence is coffee." Her praise of coffee went on, and there was in her voice even a hint that any woman who ordered juice could not be up-to-date.

The drinks arrived. Two cups of coffee. The young couple look dazed as though possessed. Miss Hyŏn pursed her lips in an "I-told-you-so" sneer and went back, filling the passage with her broad hips.

The coffee served at Sanho was, in fact, a fake. Neither black nor red in color, it gave off an unpleasantly sweet odor and had the flavor of dishwater. One gulp would make you feel like vomiting.

The long-haired cook made it. Indeed, he made it with such great confidence that if anybody complained about the quality of his product in his presence, he would retort with the theory that any cook skillful enough to make coffee that suited everybody's taste would not be rotting away at a third-class tearoom like Sanho. If you want better, why don't you go to a tourist hotel coffee shop for it and stop hanging around Sanho, he would say.

Moreover, when there were few customers he would come out to join the drinkers of his product and talk or even ask them for a cigarette.

Besides the cook, Miss Hyŏn worried Son very much. Her name was fictitious. Maybe her temper was too. She placed too much confidence in her looks. The gap between the customers' objective evaluation of her and her own subjective appraisal was great, but since she refused to recognize the former, one could hardly expect her to modify her behavior.

The cook would say that she had a "democratically" formed face, which meant that her eyes, ears, mouth and nose had taken their respective places as they pleased.

To Miss Hyŏn, the criterion upon which to measure her popularity with the customers was the number of cups of coffee she managed to "snatch" from them in a day.

To augment sales, Miss Hyŏn, while avoiding Son's eyes, would approach whomever she thought would be easy to handle and cajole them into buying her cups of coffee.

Joy alternated with sorrow, sorrow with joy, according to the number of cups of coffee she had thus "snatched" from the customers. Yesterday was a good day, worth living, since she had gotten as many as ten cups. Today five, a bad day — maybe bad enough to kill herself, she would think.

In her younger days, Miss Hyŏn dreamed of becoming a singer, not a teahouse waitress. Even now, that dream possessed her day and night and she despised those silly, fellow waitresses who, in hope of becoming a proprietress, would readily go after some rich old man.

On the dark ceiling she used to imagine herself standing on stage with the limelight bathing the length of her, singing so sweet a song that it melted every heart in the packed hall. She also dreamed that just after she had become a star, a poor, self-supporting student would appear before her, one she could devote herself to and assist.

With her help, the student would graduate from university. But the moment would come when he would betray her confidence in a grand style; he would become a judge or prosecutor or some such, and leave her.

Things had to go that way, because at the grand finale of her farewell recital she had to die on stage by taking poison, singing for the audience encores of her song "Eulogy of Death," which had been originally sung by Yun Sim-dŏk, the famous female singer who killed herself over an unrequited love affair. This was the plot of her concocted story.

The night had grown quite late. Kim Shi-ch'ŏl looked around at the other people in the room. All of them were regular customers, each occupying the seat he was accustomed to taking, killing time, in a loose, shapeless posture.

The man sitting nearest the counter was Mr Ch'ae, former chief of a newspaper branch office. He had retired a few years ago because of his involvement in a money scandal, or, according to some, an affair with a woman.

A widower in early middle age, this man found joy in life by complaining that the young newspapermen nowadays lacked the ambitious spirit their seniors had possessed, but those who knew him better talked about his having designs on Son, the proprietress. Perhaps because of this, he never failed to sit in front of the counter. He would cup his chin in his hands and steal glances at Son, all the while pretending not to watch her.

Sitting in the corner, facing Kim Shi-Ch'ŏl was Mr Ch'oe, an aging undergraduate. He had attended his university for nine years, including three years of military service.

Because of his circumstances he had to spend half of the school year earning his school expenses and the other half attending classes. Now on a leave of absence, he was working to earn his expenses. When he came to Sanho, he used to fumble in one pocket or another for a cigarette butt. His wretched condition drew upon him neglect of service by none other than Miss Hyŏn, whom he liked most.

These were the only two with whom Kim Shi-ch'ŏl had any intimacy, though it did not go beyond a mere, occasional exchange of glances in greeting. However, Kim Shi-ch'ŏl knew a great deal about the other customers as well, because Miss Hyŏn had passed on personal information about them which she had picked up, like a sparrow, as she made her rounds.

All told, the customers were either out of active service or found the times not in their favor, so they had no idea what the pleasures of life were.

Without warning, the clamor of iron plates being beaten down in the agricultural factory stopped. Instead, the voices of men fighting reached his ear. In a few minutes, as the fight began to heat up, the voices grew so loud that Kim Shi-ch'ŏl lifted the curtain which was as thick as the drapery at the entrance to a dark-room, and opened the window.

A high intensity lamp hanging from the eaves of the low U-shaped slate roof cast light over the untidy courtyard of the factory where empty drums and iron bars lay scattered.

Two men, bare to the waist, were fighting ferociously, one chasing and the other chased, the sweat on their naked muscles reflecting the bright light.

The chaser held in his hand a hammer as large as a wooden pillow, while the chased was empty-handed. Exchanging oaths and obscenities, they stalked each other through the space between the drums and around the pillars of the building.

A few fellow workers were watching them, chuckling with their arms folded.

The empty-handed man, driven at last into a corner, turned and stepped toward his pursuer. Thrusting his head forward he cried, "All right. Go ahead and hit. Hit me if you dare!" The man with the hammer held up the instrument and glared at him.

Seeing this happen before his eyes, Kim Shi-ch'ŏl felt a fresh tension overwhelm him for the first time in many days.

"Don't you know I've already chosen death before poverty? All right. Go on and hit me quickly. Then I'll have my wish," the man challenged.

The man with the hammer went through the motions of striking his instrument down fiercely. Kim Shi-ch'ŏl imagined the man's brains being smashed under the weight of the hammer. He looked forward to the moment. But the man with the hammer hesitated. Then he threw it away and began to cry. That was all.

A man of rather short stature, who seemed to be the factory manager, appeared and began to rail at them in a clear, crisp voice: "You swine. You fight every day and eat expensive rice, you have no intention of doing any good. You fools, you're all to be pitied, all leading a hard life. Yet you don't help one another. Instead you go crazy like this and beat each other up. Bastards!"

Kim Shi-ch'ŏl closed the window and lowered the curtain. He felt the tension of a moment ago still squirming inside.

Time now to go, he thought, to his boarding house

where cold rice would be waiting for him. He would never come to this teahouse again, he thought.

2

One of the same old kind of days. Nothing new. Kim Shi-ch'ŏl's letter of resignation still in his pocket. Son's white teeth and smile as usual.

Kim Shi-ch'ŏl sat and ordered coffee. He knew the quality of coffee there, of course, but no matter what he ordered, they served coffee, that he knew also. He was never at a loss what to order.

The coffee arrived. Miss Hyŏn placed it on the table, a smile about her lips. She had never smiled as she did now.

"You'll be surprised," she said.

"I am surprised already. You mean you won first place in an amateur singing contest?" Nothing surprising could happen except for something like that, he thought.

Just as Miss Hyŏn was about to answer, Son cut her off by calling, "Miss Hyŏn," and sending her the stare of a dormitory supervisor.

"You'll know soon what it is." Miss Hyŏn whispered hurriedly and turned away, a mischievous look in her eyes. Kim Shi-ch'ŏl was surprised again. Something had happened, he thought. Something important.

What that something was he knew as soon as he took a sip of the coffee. It did not taste like dishwater but like real coffee. Kim Shi-ch'ŏl came near spitting it out.

Seeing that Kim Shi-ch'ŏl had been surprised at the coffee, Son came to him. "You like it?"

"What's this change all about?"

"We have a new cook. I came upon a good cook and let Yi, the old one, go." Kim Shi-ch'ŏl turned toward the kitchen and saw an arm, as thin and white as a woman's, flit across the crescent-shaped wicket.

After the new cook came, Sanho began to change. The music was the first thing to change. In place of the plaintive "slow-slow-quick" songs Miss Hyŏn preferred to sing along with, came light, rhythmic popular songs.

Next came the curtains. The thick, dark-green wool gave way to cool, light linen curtains.

The lighting fixtures increased in number until the room became brighter. Picture frames, seat covers and such were all exchanged for new ones.

Of all the changes, however, the most shocking one was Son's attitude toward life.

"Even in adversity, we should not withdraw. We should at least find a way to amuse ourselves, even in a limited sphere. If it is too glaring to go outside, we should cultivate our inner strength so as to adapt ourselves to it. If we don't extend that bit of effort, we will fall behind for good."

Miss Hyŏn dropped a hint that all these changes had been brought about under instructions that had come from the kitchen.

All the customers tilted their heads in wonder, not so much at the new environment they had unexpectedly faced, but over the identity of the cook, who had accomplished in a few days the seemingly impossible task of toppling the twenty-year-old atmosphere of the place.

Days passed into weeks and weeks into months, but the cook never put in an appearance in the room, nor was he seen when going to the toilet.

Only his arms, thin and white as a woman's, flashed on and off inside the wicket, augmenting the customers' curiosity.

Son and Miss Hyŏn also seemed unusually united in denying any personal knowledge of the cook. They flatly refused to reveal even his name, age and place of birth. Moreover, they saw to it that nobody peeped inside the kitchen.

The customers therefore could only exchange simple guesses among themselves: since nobody had heard him say anything, he might be dumb, or he might have a great burn on his face that he did not wish to be seen.

However, one day Kim Shi-ch'ŏl happened across a strange rumor. One day when, because of the cook's case, he had begun to find the world a little interesting, so much so that he forgot to tender his resignation — that was when he heard it.

It was Mr Ch'oe, the perpetual student, who told him. Ch'oe came to Kim Shi-ch'ŏl and asked, "Have you heard the rumor, Mr Kim?"

"Well, yesterday somebody said that the cook had attended a first-rate university in Seoul. Is that what you mean?"

"So that's all you know?"

"Yes."

"Then you're still in the dark about it."

"Am I?"

"He's a fugitive, they say."

"What?"

"Hush! Don't raise your voice. He's a criminal on

the police 'Most-Wanted' list. He's hidden himself here, they say.''

''Who told you so?''

''Nobody knows the source. You remember Mr Kim, the man from Sand Control Office? He said he'd heard it from somebody. It's the information that counts, not the source of it, right?''

Mr Ch'oe appeared to be on edge, as though he himself were the fugitive wanted by the police, ready to flee at the slightest touch.

Not only Mr Ch'oe but the rest of the regulars were all on tiptoes of excitement. They sat in groups, whispering to each other and stealing glances at the kitchen.

Business at Sanho had begun to drop off.

Son, seeing the way the customers were behaving, scowled at them, pulling a long face. Miss Hyŏn kept behind the counter, as nerveless as a centipede moistened with spit. But Sanho's customers had never been so full of life.

Mr Ch'ae joined Kim Shi-ch'ŏl and Mr Ch'oe in their discussion of the case. Instead of penetrating to the pith of the rumor, they began by gnawing at the fringes, as a silkworm does to a mulberry leaf.

''What sort of crime would he have committed?'' Kim Shi-ch'ŏl led off.

''He must have brought disgrace upon himself, perhaps unintentionally,'' Ch'ae responded with confidence. ''Say, he was sent to prison on a false charge that he had killed his wife. He broke out of prison to catch the true culprit, I'm sure.''

''Damn you! That's the TV series with Richard Kimball, *The Fugitive*, isn't it?'' Ch'oe scolded him.

Ch'ae laughed awkwardly.

"My guess is that he *is* a murderer," the old undergraduate insisted.

"You're telling it!" Ch'ae cut in and went on. "He couldn't forgive the criminal acts of someone who was as mean as an insect, who exploited the poor and innocent. So he killed the old pawnbroker woman with an axe."

"I think I've heard that story too, many times," Ch'oe said.

"You've already heard it? Well, I guess I'd better not go any further," Ch'ae laughed.

"You're both too conventional in your thinking. I'm disappointed in you," Kim Shi-ch'ŏl commented.

"Then what's your unconventional way of thinking, Mr Kim?"

"I see the cook from a different angle. I take his crime in a symbolic way, not as a concrete, black-or-white one. In short, he's hiding in this teahouse under accusation of a crime at once real and unreal."

"What are you talking about? He's under false accusation, that is, you mean he's unjustly stigmatized?"

"Not exactly. What I mean is that he did certainly make a mistake. The mistake I'm talking about is that he was born extraordinary or superior. To be born superior to others means superior capability or, in a sense, superior conscience," Kim Shi-ch'ŏl explained.

"How absurd. How could such a conscience or capability be a crime?"

"It could be, of course, because a man of superior capability or superior conscience drowns those around him. Those who are ordinary or those who are snobs will find it impossible to keep up with him, even if they were to wear spiked running shoes. Then, they will surely regard that quality in him as a deadly weapon that will eventually hurt them. Could you, Mr Ch'oe, allow a man with such a deadly weapon to ride in the same boat with you?''

"I like concrete categories — a rapist, a flagrant criminal; a Communist, a thought criminal. One deserves the death penalty, the other, life imprisonment. This way of classifying crimes makes it easier for me to understand them than this theory you've developed that one is a criminal because one is superior to others. Frankly, I don't like your theory. I'd rather stand proudly on the side of convention.''

Ch'oe and Kim Shi-ch'ŏl passed several hours this way, each claiming he was closest to guessing the truth, until Son announced that the shop would close early that day.

They had to stop, but before they left, they at least agreed that the crux of the problem lay in whether or not the cook could be a felon. This even though they still had no precise idea of the nature of the crime, and of course there would be no point in searching for the weapon employed in the imagined crime either. But clearly there was something about this cook that society could not tolerate in its written or unwritten laws.

So they decided that he must be a felon, because only such a one could be so conspicuous even *incognito*, that those near him sensed they had come close to some real event. It mattered little whether he had brandished an axe or his conscience.

3

Back in his room at the boarding house, Kim Shi-ch'ŏl did not feel like eating rice. He still felt the excitement of Sanho, which was making his heart thump. He decided to put an end to his imaginings about the cook by coming once and for all to a rational conclusion. He forgot his hunger and confronted the task fervently.

As the night advanced, he had to admit that he knew nothing about the cook. He might be a nondescript, of doubtful or low origins. Why should he be a university student, though rumor said he was?

However, Kim found himself attracted to the rumor, partly because it satisfied his sense that there were concealed circumstances in the case. Take for example his mysterious power, keeping Son and Miss Hyŏn at his beck and call. They protected him from public notice with the kind of passion with which they might protect their spirit tablet jar from intruders. Though there were some gaps in his logic, Kim wanted to believe that the cook was a university student and a suspect wanted by the police.

As the night wore on, the image of the cook began to appear before his eyes. It began to change into many different sizes, like so many roasted silkworm cakes. Around midnight, the image unexpectedly turned into Atom, the space boy that appeared in the children's cartoons. Like Atom in the cartoons, the cook was as good as a superman, Kim Shi-ch'ŏl thought. Having run out of "Atrontium" or something like that, the cook, too, had been forced down and was staying just temporarily in places like Sanho, under the guise of a cook, meanwhile cultivating his strength against the day when he would ascend to the sky again to fly freely. Then, he would resume his fight with the bad guys and defeat them.

The cook's victory would be Kim's own, because the cook was Kim's agent who would do Kim's job for him, the job which had defied him, Kim Shi-ch'ŏl thought. Through the cook, Kim could be relieved. If the cook failed, Kim would fail, too. Then, he would never be able to get away from Sanho, ever.

Kim Shi-ch'ŏl was a coward who could not steal even a piece of taffy from a roadside stall or cheat on an examination. A sissy who had no guts to send in his letter of resignation to the primary school where he worked, though he had long been utterly disillusioned by the teaching profession.

Overexcited, Kim Shi-ch'ŏl passed a sleepless night.

4

The next day, a strange atmosphere permeated Sanho Tearoom. A few regular customers including Ch'oe and Ch'ae were there, all in gloomy silence. Son was nowhere in sight. Only Miss Hyŏn went about the room, swinging her hips the way she had done before the cook came. Today she had returned to her old ways.

After the cook had come to Sanho, she had appeared at the tearoom a changed person, docile and obedient. Her gait had changed and her way of laughing, too; she had walked gently and covered her mouth when she laughed. She had even blushed and been bashful. All told, she had begun to grow quite ladylike. Moreover, she had appeared full of happiness every day, a happiness that seemed to come from an inexhaustible, mythical *Hwasu* tray. She had seemed unable to contain herself and impatient to find excuses for ladling out her newfound delight.

Now she was no better than she had been before. Drinking and flirting with the customers, she threaded her way through the narrow space between the chairs. She would come to an occupied table and sit down uninvited. From time to time, she'd ask a customer to buy her a cup of whisky and tea. "A man shouldn't be a miser. Just a cup of whisky and tea, and I'll ask no more. What do you say? Shall I fill in the ticket?" she'd wheedle.

Now she came to ask Kim Shi-ch'ŏl. As soon as he nodded consent, she hurried off to the kitchen and, ignoring all normal procedures, made the tea herself and began to sip it. The cook did not appear in the kitchen, nor was his arm visible.

Mr Ch'oe, the old student, came to tell Kim the news. Tomorrow the cook would be moving on to another place. Ch'oe suggested, "Let's have a drink somewhere."

Kim felt weightless for a moment. He felt betrayed by the cook. Speechless with disappointment, he followed Mr Ch'oe. In the wine house, they exchanged cups in silence.

When the wine began to show its effect, Mr Ch'oe opened his mouth reluctantly. "That guy should not go on running from one place to another. He can't go far in this small country, can he? He's got to be caught again, I'm sure. He should settle things right here, no matter what might happen to him. It may be more heroic and honorable of him to be caught and have his say rather than to live on in humiliation. He has a sort of obligation not to disappoint those who think so highly of him, hasn't he?"

Kim Shi-ch'ŏl regretted having had a sleepless night, drawing a happy picture of himself seeking humbly for the super-power of the Atom boy. What a silly and vain dream he had had, like a cripple forcing himself to rise! Kim Shi-ch'ŏl let go a suppressed laugh. He kept on drinking, without answering.

"For his future's sake, I think it's better for somebody to tell the authorities about him," Mr Ch'oe said as he left.

After Mr Ch'oe was gone, Kim Shi-ch'ŏl trudged toward his boarding house by himself, his eyes heavy from drink.

A telephone booth came in view. He went into it and stood before the apparatus. Then, as though following a prearranged procedure, he turned the dial composedly. One, one again, then two.

He heard a couple of tones, and then the moment came when the weapon of civilization broke down the barrier of distance.

"Yes. This is one, one, two." The heavy voice of a man rang out loudly, as though it would strike him in the face. Overwhelmed by the voice, Kim Shi-ch'ŏl looked down at the receiver in his hand for a few seconds.

"Hello. Hello." Like a living thing, the receiver cried out.

With deceptive calmness, Kim Shi-ch'ŏl hung up

the receiver and quickly came out of the booth. Outside, an unpleasant, confused after-taste seized him. He was not sure whether he had said something on the phone or not.

5

It happened that night, or to be more precise, during the time between that night and daybreak of the following day.

To the small number of witnesses it seemed a perfectly grotesque incident, involving a local phone-in request program called "Midnight Song Garden". This was broadcast chiefly for those few among the citizenry who were either chronic insomniacs or who suffered occasional inability to sleep. They turned on their radios and happened to hear the following request:

"I want to hear 'Eulogy of Death,' sung by Yun Sim-dŏk."

" 'Eulogy of Death' you say — let me see. Your mere mention of the title fills my heart with a strange emotion. Do you have anyone particular in mind to whom you want to dedicate this song?"

"No. I just want to enjoy it by myself."

"I see. Will you please tell me your name and address?"

"My name is Semi. That's all I want to say about myself."

"Then I will prepare the song 'Eulogy of Death' for you. Any special reason for requesting this particular song, Miss Semi?"

Up to that point, things had gone on in an ordinary fashion, nothing unusual about it.

Then, it happened. In a tone rather agitated, yet indecent, the girl began to pour out words that would shock her listeners:

"I have just cut my artery with a knife. I feel so good, I can't tell you how much. I have been disappointed in love. I loved a poor student who was working his way through school. I loved him so much that I helped him with his tuition fees, living expenses and all! I loved him as devotedly as I could, but he betrayed me. He left me as soon as he had graduated and risen to a high position. Thank you for the song. I am enjoying it. Semi is dying quietly, thinking of your song as a funeral dirge for her last journey."

"Hello — hello. Please, wait a minute, Miss Semi. Listen to me."

Circumstances being what they were, the announcer, out of human fellowship, used every possible means to prolong contact with the girl, while he had one of his colleagues alert the police.

Once notified, the police began to trace the call, enlisting the help of the Telephone and Telegraph Office. However, it took more than two hours for them to succeed in their undertaking, and the announcer all the while had to sweat through a live broadcast of the most unusual dialogue ever heard on the airwaves.

6

Spectators were crowding around the rickety building that housed the tearoom. On the street in front a place had been roped off in a square where there lay a bloodstained straw bag that looked as if it had been tossed down haphazardly. The blood had now dried black in the sun. Shattered pieces of glass were also scattered about, reflecting the light.

It had been some time since the corpse had been carried away. But the circles and arrows drawn in white chalk on the road were still clear enough to indicate exactly where it had lain.

Primary teacher Kim Shi-ch'ŏl elbowed his way into the tearoom. The landlady of the downstairs inn was there, alone in the broad, empty room, tearing down the curtains.

She greeted him with an abstracted look. They had known each other for a long time. She said she had been summoned to the police station as a witness and had returned just now.

She continued: "At first, I was so terrified that I almost fainted. I heard a terrible crash and rushed outside. He was lying there, with blood all over. To make matters worse, he jumped out, hugging the window frame and all. To see him jump head first, he must have intended to kill himself, not to escape, I'm sure." Then, clicking her tongue, she resumed her work on the curtains.

"Why are you tearing down the new curtains?" Kim Shi-ch'ŏl asked.

"Son asked me to, when I left the station. We were there together. Not only the curtains, the ornamental lamps, too. She wanted them down and asked me to get somebody else for the job. She said something like, 'After all, a city needs shade.' "

"How about Miss Hyŏn? What's she doing?"

"You know what she's doing, don't you? She's as nonchalant and carefree as though nothing had happened. What do you suppose she did when the policemen rushed here? Cut an artery? No. They say she was pouring herself cups of wine as she talked on the phone with the radio announcer. Because of that damned act of hers an innocent soul has gone for nothing." She swore.

"Not necessarily because of Hyŏn. Who knows but somebody had turned him in?"

The landlady raised her head in disbelief. "You don't mean that," she said, looking him up and down. Her face seemed to blanch at the unexpected blow.

Kim Shi-ch'ŏl turned back and went down the creaking steps. He remembered the resignation letter he still kept in his inner pocket. He took it out and tore it up. Then he threw the shreds over the stairs as he went down. He pushed the door open and went out.

7

For days after the incident, primary teacher Kim Shi-ch'ŏl studied the newspapers, but he couldn't find anything about the cook's suicide. There was no mention of it, not the smallest article.

Translated by Ch'oe Hae-ch'un

The House of Twilight

The moment we were about to cross the road, I let go of the girl's hand when I heard the blaring of a horn coming from around the corner. An ox cart loaded with sheaves of rice that was lumbering noisily along the road barely had time to pull over to the side before a convoy of army trucks came speeding down the road with their headlights glaring yellow. A flock of baby chicks had been following the ox cart pecking at the grains that fell on the road, but they scattered. The trucks carried a battalion that had finished fighting the communist partisans in Naejang Mountain.

Instantly we were caught up in a cloud of dust. Amid the whirlwind that engulfed us in dust and grit, I opened my eyes a crack and waved my hand high toward the soldiers on the truck. But they showed no reaction to my greeting and just cast a vague glance past me as though they were not yet awake. The soldiers still had camouflage of tree branches attached to their helmets and shoulders, and their faces were all covered with a layer of yellow dust. Then one of them finally noticed me. His forehead was wrapped in bandages. He looked, then scowled, and suddenly his mouth began to twitch. Too late, I realized that this queer twisted expression was his struggle to respond to my greeting; the truck with the bitter smile was already lost in the dust and the next truck was passing in front of us. I was about to wave again when I suddenly glanced to the side. The girl was not waving. Looking as if she would die of boredom, she was waiting for the line of trucks to pass. She was clutching a small jar full of honey in her grimy hands. I'd nicked it from the kitchen pantry just earlier without Mother knowing it. The reason Kyŏng-ju did not immediately wave to the soldiers was partly because of the honey jar. But then, even when her hands were not occupied, I had never once seen her wave at the GMC's (that's what we called the trucks) when they went by. Presently, the trucks all passed by and everything returned to its original appearance under the dust. When the ox cart that had been resting on the roadside once more began to totter and clatter along, the girl and I held hands again and crossed.

One of the chicks lay squashed on the road. The tread marks of the massive truck tires were still distinct on the white feathers, and the innards had gushed from the chick's belly intact, as if someone had scooped them out. The girl stopped walking and spat on it.

The brick building that stood almost opposite our house on the other side of the highway was covered with dead ivy vines. Any way you approached it, the building looked just as though a worn-out net had been thrown over it. In the afternoons we spent most of our time inside this building. The place where we usually played was a huge furnace that had been used for melting iron. When we climbed up on top of it and looked up, far above we could see the rusted pulleys that had been used for lifting things and the sturdy beams from which dangled three or four heavy chains. And far above that, where the spider webs hung tangled at a dizzying height, was the roof, shaped like an enormous monk's hood. From the glass skylight in the center of the roof a square shaft of light poured down and stood still, like a pillar high in the darkness, illuminating each of the countless specks of dust that floated in the air. The girl sat astraddle the farthest edge of the furnace and kept smearing honey on the running sores at the corners of her mouth. I fidgeted as I sat beside her watching the gradually dwindling honey in the jar. I had taken a full one without my mother's knowing. At first the girl seemed to remember that, but once she had tasted the honey she began to ignore my concern. I hinted to her that her sores would not get better if she kept licking off the honey that she applied to them as medicine, but she did not return the jar to me until it was half empty.

"Look! Do you see that big beam there?" The girl brandished a rod and pointed upward. "My big sister hanged herself there and died."

Wielding the stick, she beat the chain hanging over her head with all her might. This was one of her bad habits. I often heard her tell me this gruesome story accompanied by the sharp metallic sound of a chain clanking against other chains as it swung slowly back and forth overhead like a clock's pendulum. When she did that, my bad molar hurt so much I could not sit still, as if I had bitten a sour apricot.

"She fought with Mother all night long, then left the house. When we looked for her in the morning, there she was, hanging from that beam. Swinging back and forth with her tongue hanging out like this."

The girl grabbed my elbow and snickered. Listening quietly to this story was a monumental task for me.

Why did the girl rattle on about her dead sister all the time? Although I had heard this repulsive story several times, Kyŏng-ju muttered on by herself as if she were passing along a rumor she had just heard to a person she had met for the first time. I had nightmares for several days after I first heard this story. I had to feel with my hands to see if my head was still attached right where it was supposed to be. At the time it was impossible for me to imagine how a person could take his own life. How her sister's neck must have hurt when the tough cord began to draw tight around it! I wanted to advise anyone please to use a gentle rope. As Kyŏng-ju described her sister's death in even more disgusting detail, she did not hesitate to say she had pooped at least twice as much as normal. I made up my mind that I should remind her that it was not the first time I had heard this story. Then she started to beat the chain again. The metallic sound had faded but now the clanking came back to life. There was nothing to do but press the tip of my tongue against my decayed tooth and try to endure it.

"There was a big commotion — it was so awful. People came running. They screamed that my sister had died. They went around the neighborhood banging a gong....But Mother was so frightened that she couldn't go outside. She couldn't budge. She just stayed in her room. It wasn't until the people came down from the mountain after burying my sister that my mother burst out crying. She cried all night long and the next day until evening...."

Instead of asking her to please stop, I just gulped down the spit in my mouth.

"The twins...You didn't know them. Before you

moved here this place was their..."

Kyŏng-ju was talking about the twin brothers who had run the iron foundry.

I had never met them, but I had heard of them from Kyŏng-ju, who knew a lot about them. The two worked as blacksmiths together, but the older of the two went into the army early and died in action, and later the younger worked the smith's hammer alone. He drank every day at the tavern Kyŏng-ju's family ran at their house. The night of the incident he was so drunk that he just slept through it snoring, without realizing that Kyŏng-ju's sister had climbed up on top of the furnace in the foundry. Even when he was helping to dig the grave in the common burial ground, his body reeked of alcohol. Not long after Kyŏng-ju's sister hanged herself, he was forging an axe when he accidentally struck his own ankle and became crippled. Not long after that, a fire broke out in his foundry and he lost almost everything. He left and went somewhere far away. And so the brick building was left there empty.

"This building is haunted by demons. The twins said so. You know what demons are, don't you?"

When she saw me shake my head, she grew all the more enthusiastic.

"Demons are...they're goblins that are created when human blood stains a broom that has been used to clean the privy."

When she finished speaking, the girl brandished the rod again. She made the chain swing like a pendulum, and let out a painful scream. I ended up missing my chance to remind Kyŏng-ju how bad her memory was.

" 'The poor girl!' That's what the grown-ups say, but it was Mother's fault that she died. It's just the same as if Mother killed her. All my mother did every day was drink and cry, so my sister tried to kill her. But since she couldn't kill Mother, she decided to go ahead and die first. Sometimes I want to kill Mother too. Every now and then. And someday I will kill her."

Kyŏng-ju's eyes glowing in the shadows made me tremble with fear. I did not doubt in the least that she could kill her own mother. She was a girl quite capable of it. Sometimes she caught mice, poured gasoline on their backs and set them on fire. They would jump around but soon died with their mouths hanging open. Kyŏng-ju watched intently during the short moment when the mouse rolled its eyes back and writhed trying to stay alive. Then she yelled. "It only managed to go one step! I thought it could have gone at least five."

And that's not all. She even pulled the feathers out of a live sparrow. Then she took the naked bird and after snapping one of its wings and both legs, she got angry and stamped her feet because it would not try to run away.

"My mouth hurts again." After chattering awhile, Kyŏng-ju was silent. Out of the corner of her eye, she kept ogling the honey jar I was holding. She scowled. "I need to put some medicine on."

She was three years older, I had no choice but to give her what honey was left.

Although it was quite some time after the incident that we had moved to Chongup, many people still devoted themselves to stories about Kyŏng-ju's family and new rumors. They had been worked up over this and that for some time. When women of the village came to our house to visit, my mother made efficient use of the stories about Kyŏng-ju's family to make friends, so we were able to find out all about their circumstances in one shot. We lived in a Japanese-style house with a steeply slanted tile roof and many windows. For a small family like ours, it was too large a house, with its spacious front garden and a backyard kitchen garden, too. In our new life that began here in Chongup, the first enemy that came to pick a fight with me was this devil with the long fingernails. Although older than I, she was shorter. Her clothes were always filthy. She hid herself between the fences or behind the electric pole, and when I came outside, she ambushed me. Wherever I went she dogged my steps waiting for a chance to scratch me. Then she rained abuse on me. She was as agile as a wildcat, and her glistening eyes told me how much she detested me.

''Thief! You son of a thief. Drop dead, you son of a thief!''

I was shocked by all the inglorious names she chanted as she dogged me, and I told my mother all about it. When we heard the explanation from the village women, we understood the reason the girl hated me as much as she did; however, my mother's darkened expression never relaxed.

''Don't go near that girl! Don't have anything to do with her!''

The house that we were living in had originally been the property of Kyŏng-ju's family. But just after the Liberation, a stranger appeared who drove out Kyŏng-ju's family and took possession of the house by some underhanded means. Kyŏng-ju's family built a

shanty next to the foundry and her mother began selling liquor. Meanwhile, the house passed through a
number of hands. Ignorant of the way things work,
Kyŏng-ju's mother regarded anyone who moved into
the house as thieves, regardless of the change in
owners, and bombarded them with incessant curses.
When I heard the stories that passed between the local
women and my mother, I decided to look for an opportunity to clear up Kyŏng-ju's misunderstanding. One
day when she drove me into a corner, I did not try
to escape. At a distance where Kyŏng-ju's hands could
not reach me, I began explaining as fast as I could talk.
I employed my tongue to the best of my ability to tell
her simply that we were not bad people and that we
had bought the house at a fair price. But standing in
front of Kyŏng-ju as she bent her ten fingers like a rake
and waited for her chance, things only got worse as
I fumbled for words. Finally, not only was I unable to
explain in simple terms, I got confused myself about
what I was talking about. Kyŏng-ju did not let me finish
what I had to say. Flying into a rage like a fire blazing,
she brandished her rake-like fingernails. But before she
could tear at the meat she suddenly withdrew her
hands and laughed. Then she gave me a perplexingly
hospitable look. Had she understood what I said? I
wanted to believe that perhaps she had understood.
But if she had then finally realized that we were good
people, it was not just thanks to my awkward persuasion. My ludicrous efforts, as I sweated all flustered
and confused, must have looked very commendable
in her eyes. At any rate, after this incident we became
good friends, and Kyŏng-ju started stealing old stiff
bond certificates that had faded red and giving them

to me as a token of her trust in my kindness and obedience.

If only Kyŏng-ju could have erased her big sister's death from her memory, the sooty inside of the iron foundry would have been a more pleasant place. There were all kinds of ironware buried in the ashes. If you had a mind to, you could find the unfinished axe head right where the younger twin had been working on it. If you poked around with your foot, you could turn up all sizes of metal weights, sets of hinges, and things like the stump of a sickle, a kitchen knife, or a horseshoe. Once we found these things, we enjoyed burying each of them again in a place different from where we had found them, in preparation for the next day's play.

A huge pair of tough leather bellows lay in front of the firehole of the furnace. The pine boards that formed the body were rotten and the leather had holes burned in it, so when you grasped the handles and pushed, instead of a wind, it made an uncanny sound like an old man breathing. It was quite a curiosity. There was also a half-burned ash rake that we used to pile the ashes together into a mountain. We got black all over. The passing breeze blew inside, rattling the broken windows and making us smell the moist odor of the mildew that we had forgotten for a while. As time passed, the square pillar of light crept imperceptibly toward our feet, illuminating slantwise the interior of the dark, damp building. Finally the sun would drop low in the sky, and we could hear distinctly the sound of the sparrows that had returned from the fields as they chased each other about on the roof and pecked with their delicate beaks on the gutters at the eaves. Sometimes they also hopped up and down the ivy vines on the outside wall, beating their wings as they went. They did this in summer too, but once autumn came the vines that seemed to veil the old building looked all the more gaunt. They said the vines used to cover the whole brick building with heavy, green leaves, but people said that after the fire the ivy had probably all died and would not bud again when spring came.

Sunset. it was a fearful time, yet a time of day that enveloped me in an excitement and curiosity that clung to me. Occasionally as the sunset blazed on the glass, I gazed at the window of the tavern that Kyŏng-ju's family ran. I would gradually end up submerged in a weird inescapable fantasy. I cannot really say what caused me to feel this way. But from the first moment I saw this house, I immediately sensed a peculiar atmosphere, something like a dark, dank odor that surrounded it. After the vague guesses I had pieced together from the dropped hints of the neighbors had been confirmed, I felt some mysterious power that seemed to wrap around me, and I fell into the habit of secretly expecting that some bizarre event I could not comprehend would once again occur there. Compared to the dilapidated condition of Kyŏng-ju's house, surrounded by its earthen wall and covered with a tin roof, the glass in the window looked far too extravagant as it reflected the sunset glow. Every time I gazed at that window, I was reminded of the cavernous holes of window frames that were left in the brick walls of the foundry, and I imagined things that I should be sorry to Kyŏng-ju's family for thinking. But then a few days later, Kyŏng-ju herself confirmed the accuracy of what I had presumed. A grimy cotton shop curtain hung halfway over the entrance to the tavern where adults had to hunch over to go inside. There was written in poor hand *makkŏli*, *yakju*, and the names of a couple of coarse dishes. Whatever time of day you looked in, business appeared slack. The vendors who came on market days, the people from distant places, and most of the boozers in the village dropped in at Kyŏng-ju's house for just a short while, but they still got quite drunk. When there were customers, the pleasant smell of *pindaeddŏk* and *pukkumi* cakes cooking on the griddle drifted out with the white steam through the shop curtain. But on the days when no customers came, in the still evening, I often caught sight of the gray image of Kyŏng-ju's mother at the window as she gazed vacantly at the sky. This was an omen that her crying would begin. Kyŏng-ju's mother's face was so withered and wrinkled and her hair so gray that it seemed more appropriate to call her "Grandmother" than "Mother." And people actually did call this woman "Grandma." Grandma's crying had a fixed time to it — if not every three days, then at least every four, and sometimes without even letting a day pass for several days on end. When the red sunlight that appeared to envelop the house in flames began to gleam on the window, Grandma looked up at the sky and wailed in a wretched voice. It began with a long sharp cry, like the voice of a fox. Her wailing was so continuous, with no bottom and no end, that it sounded as though she was resorting to wiles, purposely seeking the help of anyone who might hear. It also sounded as though she might be rebuking someone. One could imagine it to be the ghastly scream that naturally flowed from the lips of a person suffering pain that would not cease. Whenever I heard her cry, my decayed tooth ached so much I could not stand it. At first I used to think the reason Grandma's face was always red was because of the liquor she was drinking all the time, but gradually I came to believe that it was because of the setting sun and the evening glow that reflected on the window; the light had dyed her face and the color would not fade from it.

"She's started again." My mother clicked her tongue when she heard the woman crying. She had also clicked her tongue when she heard from the village women the reason for the crying. She clicked her tongue about everything connected with Kyŏng-ju's family. From what I had heard, Grandma was crying because of her son, who had joined the communist partisans and had not returned. The unsparing affection that this woman had for her only son had made him a Communist. Also, her oldest daughter hated her mother so much because of her crying she wanted to kill her. So you could say that it was her brother's fault that the daughter finally killed herself. I could not quite determine whether there was any plausible or logical connection between these fragments of stories. I listened with profound interest to the explanations why Kyŏng-ju's oldest sister was forced to do what she did. She had gone looking for someone who could help her try to get her brother, who had become a communist "mountain man," to turn himself in to the authorities. But she had met up with a swindler and come home without her underwear and covered with blood. At dawn the next day, she had climbed onto the furnace. Unravelling the complicated family circumstances surrounding the death of Kyŏng-ju's eldest sister remained a difficult mental task for me. Although Kyŏng-ju usually rattled on about all kinds of things that went on in her house, for some reason, she never said a word about her older brother. A partisan had once crept into our village under cover of darkness to visit his family, but was discovered by the police and shot in the leg before he fled back to the mountains. I knew it was rumored to have been Kyŏng-ju's brother.

Kyŏng-ju also never spoke of her second sister, Kyŏng-ok. She was tall, like a Westerner, and had an attractive face and a fine figure. She cared little about what happened to her family, spending every day out in the company of men. You might say she was the carefree grasshopper who spent the whole summer singing. Her sleek, bright smile looked as though it had been greased, and it invited the disgust of the villagers. She seemed to be well aware of their feelings, but this girl always wore an expression of self-confidence. When the villagers whispered and cast furtive sidelong glances at her, her chin jutted out with a haughty air and she looked as though she were lifting her face from beneath the water to take a breath.

The faces of the men she kept company with seemed to change almost every day. The women pointed to Kyŏng-ju's sister and called her a whore. Behind her back, they scorned her as no better than a female dog. My mother looked away indifferently and clicked her tongue. The place where Kyŏng-ju's sister usually parted with her men was in the shadows of the hedge around our house. My hearing was so keen even when I was asleep that I awoke to the sound of laughter on the other side of the hedge even in the middle of the night. It happened quite seldom, but occasionally Kyŏng-ju's sister came home alone at night along this road. When she did, she was always drunk and staggering. As she walked down the deserted road, she hummed a song to herself quietly. It was a simple melody, without many high or low notes, connected by long breaths. Whenever she happened to see me from the road, she would pat the rouge on both cheeks with her fingers and stick her tongue out at me. Not once did words pass between us, but in our own peculiar, secret way, we conspired and exchanged greetings. Particularly on nights when she came home alone and saw me standing at the threshold of the door, she cackled and blew a kiss to me across the hedge. One night I saw Kyŏng-ju's sister in a dream. She was rubbing her hand over the head of some child and singing a lullaby. When I awoke, I realized that the child had been me and that the child in my dream had called Kyŏng-ok "sister." Even though I was alone, I blushed.

The day before the Harvest Moon Festival, Kyŏng-ju's sister left home.

The tavern was closed. On the day of the festival Kyŏng-ju ate breakfast at our house. Even though it was a holiday, Kyŏng-ju's family did not cook anything. My mother sent me to deliver dishes of dumplings and rice to Kyŏng-ju's mother. Through the morning, the women in the village did not realize what had happened at Kyŏng-ju's house. If they had not seen me delivering a second round of dishes at lunchtime, they would not have known anything until the next day or even the day after. They finally sensed something was out of the ordinary and began to wonder what was going on. They stopped Kyŏng-ju and asked her what had happened. Kyŏng-ju would not open her mouth, so they brought out a plate of appetizing rice cakes as bait. Kyŏng-ju hesitated for only a moment, then readily lifted her hands to accept this trifling temptation. Their curiosity relieved, the women began to talk amongst themselves about how it was only natural that it should have happened and how Kyŏng-ok had finally revealed herself to be a slut. While they passed their judgment on the girl who had left home, Kyŏng-ju was gobbling down the sticky rice cake that she had been swindled into trading for her family's secret.

Kyŏng-ju's mother did not touch the food I brought. When I opened the door to bring in lunch, the breakfast dishes I had brought earlier were still sitting there covered with a cloth just as I had left them that morning. When I looked in again later, the two piles of dishes were still there untouched. I looked at Grandma lying as though dead facing the wall on the warmer part of the floor, and I waited for Kyŏng-ju to say something. But Kyŏng-ju slammed the door shut. Inside I could hear Grandma stirring.

"Kyŏng-ok, is that you?"

That afternoon, Kyŏng-ju had brought out a big magnifying glass from somewhere and was amusing herself by burning ants with it. The autumn sun beat down on the vacant lot near the foundry where the weeds had grown dense. The ants were dying one by one, falling under Kyŏng-ju's aim as they ran busily about in the dry grass. As the number of dead ants increased, a sinister smile appeared on Kyŏng-ju's lips.

At first I had no desire to join in this new entertainment; however, I gradually began to feel a sense of pleasure watching the ants. They scurried among the leaves trying to hide themselves to escape the focus of Kyŏng-ju's pursuing magnifying glass, then mindlessly dashed out again only to end up writhing and rolling up in little balls. The ants looked as big as cabbage bugs when they appeared magnified in the glass. The oily black luster of the round abdomen made them look as though they had been washed in water, while the smaller thorax was covered with soft fuzz. When Kyŏng-ju held out the lens, the ground grew suddenly brighter and the ants were so bewildered that they did not move. Then, as the wide halo of light gradually drew in to the size of a grain of rice, they took off in a flurry. With ever so much composure, Kyŏng-ju kept the lens at the same height to maintain the focus and followed them about with a leisurely air. Before I knew it, I had become her accomplice. I did not hesitate to offer to help. Kyŏng-ju pointed out the objects of her murderous intent, then I quickly drew a circle on the ground about the size of a serving tray. We decided the conditions of the game: we would let an ant live if it ran outside the circle I had drawn. But Kyŏng-ju seldom missed. While she was haughtily tracking down her next victim, I picked up the dead ant and put it with the others. Before I knew it, beads of sweat had formed on the tip of Kyŏng-ju's nose, and I had to wipe my forehead with my sleeve. We found the anthill and beat it down. As we toyed with the ants as they squirmed out of the anthill, I savored the pompous sensation as if I had become a god. It was a difficult, annoying task to choose one particularly detestable fellow among these many identical ants, so we selected our prey according to whimsy — how we felt at the moment. Once we had sighted our victim, no matter how much it struggled, it wound up dead. We killed and killed and killed again until the sun started to go down and it became difficult to focus the light. If we had not heard Kyŏng-ju's mother crying we might have used some other method besides the lens to prolong our playing at god.

It was almost sunset. Grandma's piercing cries suddenly made us aware that the day had passed without our realizing it, and that a dark, clammy, clinging world unlike the one we knew in the daylight was about to open up before us. I gazed vacantly at one patch of reddish cloud that was sliding away beyond the roof of my house directly across the road. All at once Kyŏng-ju flung the magnifying glass away. "I'm gonna kill her! I'm gonna kill her!" she said over and over as she shot off like an arrow.

I followed after her. I thought for a moment and realized that Kyŏng-ju was empty-handed. I felt uneasy and I studied Kyŏng-ju's expression. Until then I had had no doubt that Kyŏng-ju had the ability to kill her own mother — she was such a capable child. Still, her mother was an adult. Although she was old, it would be hard for Kyŏng-ju to do it with her bare hands. I felt queasy when I thought about it. A length of cord! I kept trying to think of some kind of soft cord as I ran along out of breath. That old silk necktie of my father's would be just right! When we had almost reached the front of the tavern, I could not bear it any longer. I called to Kyŏng-ju to stop. She stood there stupefied for a moment, listening to my panted explanation. But in the next instant, her knife-like fingernails began to claw and scratch at my eyelids and cheeks. Her eyes were bloodshot and she grew furious as though she intended to begin her killing with me. I had not expected such. I had never imagined that she would come at me this way, so I could only stand there dumbfounded. I sensed vaguely that there was something mistaken in my sense of complicity that had made me stick so close to Kyŏng-ju all afternoon.

When I stood at the threshold of my own house, I could see the window of Kyŏng-ju's family's tavern clearly beyond the hedge. When I stood up on the frame I could see even better; Kyŏng-ju, small as she was, was trying with all her might to close the window that faced the road. Grandma's gaunt arm was caught in the narrow gap between the wall and the window and was dangling there. Kyŏng-ju was hunched over, pushing the window with all the strength she had, trying to eliminate even the last bit of space that her mother's arm occupied. And all the while her mother's cries did not cease. The sunlight reflecting on the window was so dazzling I could not see Grandma's face at all. From where I was I could no longer see the sun. But within the tavern window another sun still remained, and in an instant it brandished its fierce light in all directions as if to set the whole house ablaze.

"Die! Die!" Kyŏng-ju screeched and pushed even more forcefully. But the black space that kept biting and swaying like the mouth of a demon at the old woman's arm as gaunt as a vine did not narrow by so much as an inch, and her long, loud, ghastly cries did not abate. When I heard them, my molar ached so much I could not stand it, as though I were chewing a sour apricot; nevertheless, I had no thought of covering my ears.

"I'll kill you! I'll kill you! I'll kill you! I'll kill you! I'll kill you!"

The mother and daughter's battle did not stop until the sunset glow had completely faded and everything had melted into darkness. The long echoes of Grandma's cries trailed off endlessly into the black night sky. At last Kyŏng-ju plopped down on the dirt floor, exasperated, and burst out crying in a voice like her mother's. As I observed this scene, I could no longer understand what was what. What was going on? It had begun with Kyŏng-ju's mother howling when the sky turned red. The window was closed and then Kyŏng-ju's mother's form was hidden beyond the glass, only her vine-like arm appearing from the gap. She screamed that it hurt, and a moment later she began to cry at the sound of the glass that reflected the sunset being broken. Afterward they licked each other's wounds like two animals and cried until dark, in voices somewhat louder and longer than human. By then their voices did not sound in the least bit sorrowful. It struck me as a song of joy that they enjoyed on a regular basis, matching a particular melody and rhythm.

Overcome by drowsiness, I fell asleep. The first thing I did when I awoke at dawn the next morning was to see what was going on at the tavern. It was deathly still. I waited for it to get light, then I dashed over. The fog was heavy. The place was as quiet as a tomb. The fog that had descended during the night blanketed the tavern. It was an uncanny scene. With trembling hands I stealthily opened the outer gate. The smell of liquor struck my nose. I felt my heart beating louder and louder as I listened toward the living room. But the only thing I could hear from within the room was, of course, the beating of my own heart. I went around the narrow tavern counter and crept toward the living quarters. Just then, there was a clatter at my feet. I had kicked a liquor kettle with my toe and it went rolling across the floor. Broken vessels and shards of porcelain scattered about in wild disorder.

"Is that Kyŏng-ok?" A hoarse low voice escaped from the room. The door rattled open. In my bewilderment I shrieked. Grandma, her stiff, wirelike gray hair sticking out all over, had barely managed to stand up, supporting herself against the door post. At the sight of her I was dumbfounded and began to tremble. Her withered, misshapen breasts were visible through the opening in her blouse where the tie had come off. Her skirt, so dirty I could not tell whether it was originally black or white, was wrinkled terribly. Her face was as white as a sheet of paper, and there were gruesome scratches here and there. Tears had dried on her cheek and above them, her bloodshot eyes were covered with a thick discharge resembling sugar that had dissolved in the mouth. She stared at me for a moment with these eyes, then suddenly she grinned.

"Oh, you've come back home!" she cried out opening her arms as if to welcome me into the house. "You've really come back home! I'm so thankful, Kyŏng-ok. Come on inside. I was wrong. Please come on in."

When I saw Grandma stepping down to the counter, her arms spread open wide, I began to creep backwards. She kept grinning and rattling on with her honeyed words. Her acrid breath reeked of alcohol.

"I did the wrong thing. I won't cry any more. Please don't leave. Kyŏng-ok, please forgive your old mother."

Kyŏng-ju then came flying out of the inner room like a bullet. She shoved her mother aside and tried to run past her. Until then, Grandma had been staggering, unable to walk straight, but, with unbelievable agility, she seized her daughter by her long hair. Then, with just as unbelievably fearsome strength, she flung her daughter back into the corner of the room. Kyŏng-ju came flying out once more, but she was seized again. As I watched, Kyŏng-ju tried to rush out the door four times, and four times she was tossed back into the corner of the room. I dashed out the gate and fled desperately toward my house. Grandma's piercing howls followed behind me.

"Where are you going...leaving your mother? Where are you going, you bitch?"

Late in the afternoon of the next day, the weather began to turn cloudy. My father looked up at the overcast sky. In an angry voice, he was fretting over the field work he had to do. He said if the fall rains were to come soon, it would be hard to gather in the grain he had already gone to the trouble to cut. However, since the land we farmed was hardly more than a handful, my father's concern about the rains did not sound in the least appropriate. At the end of this pointless conversation, my mother and father turned their gaze toward Kyŏng-ju's house. Just a moment earlier, the two of them had been talking about Kyŏng-ju and her mother. My father pressed his hands together and rubbed them. Someone had to do something about it, he muttered. After every remark, my mother clicked her tongue. She implored me not to go anywhere near Kyŏng-ju's house.

Because of the overcast sky, I could not see the sunlight that burned in the window glass of Kyŏng-ju's house. And perhaps that was the reason I did not hear her mother crying. It had been three days. No smoke had appeared from the chimney of Kyŏng-ju's house for three days. And for three days, Kyŏng-ju and her mother had shut themselves up inside. When I looked at the tavern house and could hear no sound, I had the dreadful thought that Kyŏng-ju and her mother had eaten each other up. Enticed by my groundless imaginings, I finally ignored my mother's request.

When she noticed that someone had come inside, Grandma called out before she opened the door to her room. "Is it you, Kyŏng-ok?" But she realized that it was only me. "The kid from the tile-roofed house. The kid from the tile-roofed house...," she muttered to herself and gave me a cold glare. I wanted to hurry back outside, but, worried about Kyŏng-ju, I hesitated. I could not see her. When Grandma noticed me craning my neck to see inside the room, her attitude changed.

"Come inside for a visit. Kyŏng-ju has been sick in bed." Grandma whispered in an affected voice. She stepped back from the door to make room for me to come inside. I wavered for a moment, but she grabbed my hands, and I was dragged to the place near the fire where Kyŏng-ju was lying on the floor. The kerosene lamp dimly illuminated the disordered room. Grandma turned up the wick, and the room grew brighter.

Kyŏng-ju was lying without a cover, her eyes closed.
Immediately I saw in Kyŏng-ju's cheeks the sunset glow
that had vanished from the window. There were black
scabs on her parched lips, and every time she exhaled,
an odor like boiling soy sauce escaped. All of a sudden I was seized by a dreadful thought. I leapt up.

"Why are you leaving so soon?"

I heard the click of the door being locked.
Grandma's two sunken eyes danced slyly before me.

"Relax and stay a while before you go," she said
stroking my head.

I began to pout and cry. But she was tenacious;
a moment later she had made me sit by Kyŏng-ju's
head. Grandma rummaged through an old chest of
drawers and pulled out a wooden stationery case — a
beautiful box inlaid with mother of pearl in a floral
design. It was filled with bundles of bond certificates.
With what seemed like reluctance, she hesitated a
moment, then handed me one of the papers.

"It's money. Take it."

There had been a time when I was convinced it
really was money — the first time Kyŏng-ju gave me
one. But my mother explained that it was not money.
She told me that these papers passed for money when
the Japanese had been here, but now they were good
for nothing. I knew it was no more than a scrap of
paper, so I did not take it. Looking even more reluctant, she slipped two into my hand.

"You can buy anything you want. This is really
money. Take it."

I did not accept them. Grandma grew nervous.
Before my eyes, the number of certificates grew one
by one. I cried some more. Ungrudgingly, she began

to hand me more and more. In a moment all the bonds in the box had been placed in my hands.

Sometime earlier large drops of rains had begun beating on the tin roof. I was not satisfied with the certificates. Grandma rifled through the drawers again and arranged all kinds of things before me. Among them was a photograph album. She pointed to a man in a yellowed family portrait and told me that it was Kyŏng-ju's father. He had a moustache and was dressed in strange clothes and wore a long sword at his side. I pointed to a photograph of a beautiful young woman. Grandma struck her chest with her fist and laughed. "That's me."

Grandma pulled out another photograph and showed me an even younger woman. "Take a good look. That's a picture of me too."

Then she looked up at the ceiling, imitating the elegant smile of a refined lady.

Kyŏng-ju resembled her oldest sister in the photograph. I looked back and forth, comparing Grandma's wrinkled face with the woman in the picture. Somehow, it just seemed that she was lying. I was able to pick out Kyŏng-ju's brother, whom I had never met. He was a little boy in a sailor suit. And Kyŏng-ju was a nursing baby then.

The clamor of the rain on the tin roof grew. The roof rattled like a dry pot of beans on a hot stove. The sound of the window frames and the conduit pipes rattling in the wind in the abandoned iron foundry where that blood-covered broom hung was close enough to touch. All the while, Kyŏng-ju never opened her eyes. She seemed unaware that I had come. I cried louder. I wanted to go home. There was nothing in that room that could buy my favor. But Grandma grew fidgety trying somehow to detain me. All of a sudden she opened the door into the tavern and ran out. Then she scraped the bottom of the liquor jug, poured a bowl full of *makkŏli* and came back.

"Drink this. Drink it! I said drink it!"

I desperately tried to avoid drinking the liquor, clamping my lips shut and shaking my head; however, she twisted my nose and I ended up opening my mouth. This way she poured a bowlful down me. My stomach swelled like a tadpole's, my breath came fast, and my whole body burned like fire. I felt as though I were on a giant swing, piercing the roof and riding into the sky, then sinking down deep into the earth only to blaze up again and again.

"Sing a song," Grandma shrieked.

Kyŏng-ju opened her eyes and looked around the room. Just then Grandma increased her vigor. "A song! Sing a song to wake up Kyŏng-ju. Sing a song to make her smile. Sing!"

That night I got drunk for the first time in my life and acted disgracefully. Following Grandma's orders, I sang all the songs I had learned at school as they came to mind. I even danced about. And finally Grandma had to help me as I vomited into the chamber pot. The next day I had no memory of it. I did not even know when my father broke the door down, came and fought with Grandma. I was dead drunk.

The next morning I woke and saw Kyŏng-ju lying beside me. My mother was changing the damp cloth on Kyŏng-ju's forehead. Her body was like a mass of flames. Whenever she groaned, it smelled of soy sauce. It was still dark outside. I could hear rain falling. Within the sound, I could occasionally detect a hoarse cry. It was probably outside our gate.

"Give her back! Give back my daughter! Give her back!"

My father was puffing at his cigarette, with a look of indifference. But actually, he was quite angry. His eyes were swollen as though he had not slept a wink all night. My mother looked the same. She glared down at me reproachfully out of the corner of her eye. I was able to guess roughly what had happened. Grandma had been screaming all night long for my parents to give back her daughter, whom they had stolen away. Outside, her voice maintained its vigor, neither increasing nor decreasing, as the autumn rain continued to fall.

After the doctor left in the morning, Kyŏng-ju was able to get down a few mouthfuls of rice gruel. She was still not well enough to let us feel easy about her. Even so, compared to the previous night, she seemed to be feeling much better. The village women came, and all praised my father for taking Kyŏng-ju to our house. They told him he had handled it well. My mother's face finally brightened. Before the dawn came, Grandma had gone off somewhere, and the village grew quiet.

But a little later, Grandma appeared again and all the spectators made it look like a market had been opened in front of our gate. Grandma was a different woman now. She had wound a length of rotten straw rope on top of her head the way women do to balance loads. She was looking at herself in a broken mirror, grinning for no reason. She had changed into clean clothes that looked rather decent, but her gray hair was drenched and dishevelled, and she was barefoot as well. Grandma rolled her eyes and tried teasing the people gathered there, muttering all along. As the little kids in the village ran about in circles, they made fun of her. One stiff certificate appeared from within the front of her blouse. She flipped it into the air with a graceful movement of her hands that made her look as though she were dancing. The children pushed and fought among themselves trying to get it. Grandma screamed with laughter and tossed out another. Mindless of the rain that kept falling, everyone laughed together as they watched. Then a convoy of GMCs appeared, their horns blaring. The soldiers in the trucks stuck their heads out and watched Grandma's antics. As soon as the people got out of the way, the GMCs full of soldiers passed one by one heading toward Nae-jang Mountain. After she had scattered the bonds one at a time with graceful movements to the children who clamored around her, Grandma clapped her hands and laughed. One of the notorious village urchins put his hand into Grandma's bosom. His name was In-gi. Just as he pulled out a bundle of certificates, Kyŏng-ju, whom we had thought was sleeping inside the house, suddenly rushed out from among the crowd. She instantly grabbed In-gi and they tumbled to the ground. At that moment the papers that spilled from Grandma's breast were strewn in all directions. Kyŏng-ju and In-gi were like muddy dogs. As they rolled around where the bonds had scattered, they clawed and beat and bit each other. From the back of the spectators my mother screamed. She shouted that if someone did not do something the girl would die. But no one tried to stop them. As Grandma scattered the remaining certificates over the two fighting children, she held her stomach and laughed. Kyŏng-ju was not well, so it took her a while to beat In-gi, who normally would have been no match for her. But even though she had won, she could not get up when it was over.

Grandma just stood there looking down at Kyŏng-ju lying collapsed on the ground. Someone shouted. "She's your daughter, isn't she?" Grandma sobbed as she lifted her.

The people began to disperse one or two at a time. Someone was brushing off his clothes wet from the drizzle and grumbling as he looked at the sky. Everyone was soaked from the rain.

That was the last time I saw Kyŏng-ju and Grandma. That evening the rumble of artillery grew as the darkness settled in. Fighting had broken out in the nearby mountains, so we had to spend the whole night with our eyes wide open in the blackout. Stray bullets came flying in and their tense report rent the darkness. In the middle of the night, from under my covers, I heard the clamor of something falling down. When I looked out the next morning, Kyŏng-ju's tavern house had caved in. I was kept inside unable to go anywhere while the villagers came out with picks and shovels to dig through the collapsed house. Mother would not open the gate, saying a child should not see such things. I never saw Grandma or Kyŏng-ju again after that. My mother told me that the two of them had followed some young man and gone off to a distant place. I heard that someone had seen Grandma's son that night at the entrance to the village. It was rumored that someone had even given him a light for his cigarette. So, although I was disappointed, there was nothing to do but believe what my mother had told me about where they had gone.

Now I would never again see the sunset reflected in the window of the tavern house. Instead, when spring came the next year, the ivy I thought had been burnt to death surprised me by awakening after a long convalescence. One day when the whole brick building shone green, covered with luxuriant leaves, I could not stand my mother's nagging. I pulled my left molar that had given me so much trouble for so long and threw it onto the roof of our house. After that the village women often came to our house to visit, but there was no one who would bring up the subject of Kyŏng-ju's family. As I waited for a magpie to bring me a new tooth, my mother and the neighborhood women, before I knew it, were talking in whispers about the misconduct of a new bride who had recently moved into the village.

Translated by Martin Holman

About the Translators

Ch'oe Hae-ch'un, a native of Pusan, Korea, was a professor of English at Donga University there. His translations of Korean literature include works by Hwang Sun-won and Na To-hyang. At the time of his death in February 1989, he was completing work on a major innovative Korean-English dictionary which will be published soon.

Bruce Fulton, a former Peace Corps volunteer in Korea, received his masters degree in Korean Area Studies from the University of Washington.

Ju-Chan Fulton, a graduate of Ehwa Womens University in Seoul, received her Masters in Special Education from the University of Washington. Together the Fultons have translated a number of works of Korean literature, including stories by Hwang Sun-won published by Readers International and a forthcoming collection of stories by Korean women writers to be published by Seal Press.

Martin Holman, a graduate of Brigham Young University and a Ph.D. candidate at the University of California at Berkeley, currently teaches Japanese and Korean literature at Wakayama University near Osaka, Japan. His translations include works by Hwang Sun-won, Ibuse Masuji, and Kawabata Yasunari's *The Old Capital* and *Palm-of-the-Hand Stories*. He edited and introduced the collection *The Book of Masks*, stories by Hwang Sun-won, published by Readers International.

Suh Ji-moon, a professor of English at Korea University in Seoul, received her Ph.D. from the State University of New York at Albany. She has also studied and taught at the School of Oriental and African Studies at the University of London and at Harvard University. Her translations from Korean include *The Rainy Spell* (1983), the UNESCO Representative Collection of modern Korean stories, and stories by Hwang Sun-won published in the 1989 Readers International collection, *The Book of Masks*. She also recently published a collection of her own essays in English entitled *Faces in the Well*.

READ THE WORLD—Books from Readers International

Nicaragua	**To Bury Our Fathers**	Sergio Ramírez	£5.95/US$8.95
Nicaragua	**Stories**	Sergio Ramírez	£3.95/US$7.95
Chile	**I Dreamt the Snow Was Burning**	Antonio Skármeta	£4.95/US$7.95
Brazil	**The Land**	Antônio Torres	£3.95/US$7.95
Argentina	**Mothers and Shadows**	Marta Traba	£3.95/US$7.95
Argentina	**A Funny Dirty Little War**	Osvaldo Soriano	£3.95/US$6.95
Uruguay	**El Infierno**	C. Martínez Moreno	£4.95/US$8.95
Haiti	**Cathedral of the August Heat**	Pierre Clitandre	£4.95/US$8.95
Congo	**The Laughing Cry**	Henri Lopes	£4.95/US$8.95
Angola	**The World of 'Mestre' Tamoda**	Uanhenga Xitu	£4.95/US$8.95
S. Africa	**Fools and Other Stories**	Njabulo Ndebele	USA only $8.95
S. Africa	**Renewal Time**	Es'kia Mphahlele	£4.95/US$8.95
S. Africa	**Hajji Musa and the Hindu Fire-Walker**	Ahmed Essop	£4.95/US$8.95
Iran	**The Ayatollah and I**	Hadi Khorsandi	£3.95/US$7.95
Philippines	**Awaiting Trespass**	Linda Ty-Casper	£3.95/US$7.95
Philippines	**Wings of Stone**	Linda Ty-Casper	£4.95/US$8.95
Japan	**Fire from the Ashes**	ed. Kenzaburō Ōe	£3.50 UK only
China	**The Gourmet**	Lu Wenfu	£4.95/US$8.95
India	**The World Elsewhere**	Nirmal Verma	hbk only £9.95/US$16.95
Poland	**Poland Under Black Light**	Janusz Anderman	£3.95/US$6.95
Poland	**The Edge of the World**	Janusz Anderman	£3.95/US$7.95
Czech.	**My Merry Mornings**	Ivan Klíma	£4.95/US$7.95
Czech.	**A Cup of Coffee with My Interrogator**	Ludvík Vaculík	£3.95/US$7.95
E. Germany	**Flight of Ashes**	Monika Maron	£4.95/US$8.95
E. Germany	**The Defector**	Monika Maron	£4.95/US$8.95
USSR	**The Queue**	Vladimir Sorokin	£4.95/US$8.95

Order through your local bookshop, or direct from the publisher. Most titles also available in hardcover. *How to order:* Send your name, address, order and payment to

RI, 8 Strathray Gardens, London NW3 4NY, UK

or **RI**, P.O. Box 959, Columbia, LA 71418, USA

Please enclose payment to the value of the cover price plus 10% of the total amount for postage and packing. (Canadians add 20% to US prices.)